Down Is Out

By Mark W. Burris

This book is a work of fiction. Any resemblance to actual events or persons, living or dead, is entirely coincidental.

"Down is Out," by Mark W. Burris. ISBN 978-1-62137-084-0 (softcover), 978-1-62137-085-7 (hardcover), 978-1-62137-086-4 (eBook).

Published 2012 by Virtualbookworm.com Publishing Inc., P.O. Box 9949, College Station, TX 77842, US. ©2012, Mark W. Burris. All rights reserved. No part of this publication may be reproduced, stored in a retrieval system, or transmitted in any form or by any means, electronic, mechanical, recording or otherwise, without the prior written permission of Mark W. Burris.

Manufactured in the United States of America.

To my parents, Wayne and Avanelle, for their love and encouragement;

To my sister Sarah and her husband Tommy and their children Sam and Ben for their love and encouragement (and pizza!);

To Tom for copyediting help and invaluable advice;

To my friends—especially Bill and Carolyn and PJ—for their support, friendship and good times.

Chapter 1

Jon Prospero stared at the drop of cold rain hanging from his fingertip. He shivered, and watched the drop fall onto his boot. He wiggled his numb toes, and thought of summer. He sat hunched over a fiberoptic conduit, soaked to the skin, thinking of home, hearth, and better days.

Why was it always rainy and cold on stakeouts? He flicked another drop of rain off his nose, glanced at his watch, then checked his equipment again.

Jon's team had been watching this suspect for over a month – meticulously gathering information needed to detain, arrest, and convict. Three weeks ago, he had impersonated a telecom repairman – a natural role for him, since before he had joined the force, he had been a lineman in the Outer Territories.

Jon smiled at the memory – he had requested the assignment because it had paid so well. He had even persuaded his new wife, Lara, that it all would be fun – running around the Outback – he helping to build the infrastructure of a brand new territory, and she continuing her legal education via remote hyperlink – no messy distractions, no traffic, no high-rise vertigo, no expensive restaurants, no shows, no expensive shopping meccas. Just lots and lots of wide open spaces, clean air, beautiful starry night skies, the aroma of barbecue on the outdoor grill...

His earphone chirped faintly, bringing Jon out of his reverie – an incoming call on the team channel.

"Prospero here. Go ahead."

The gravelly voice of the stakeout lead, Nile Gryphon, came on the line. "Wet enough for ya?"

Jon grimaced. "Nile, you didn't tell me to suit up for an underwater gig."

The older man laughed. "We don't control the weather. That's Infrastructure's job."

"They must not like us too much," John said sourly.

Gryphon snorted. "Nothing I can do about it. Any sign of our boy?"

Jon checked his equipment. "Nothing in the past two hours. He's either asleep or he's snuck out again."

"Infrared shows he's definitely in there. Heat signature indicates he's asleep."

"Alone?" Jon asked.

"'Course he's alone, he's a data thief."

Jon nodded. Data thieves were by definition loners, either by inclination or social ineptness. It was a shame, really – if these people had chosen to apply their intelligence in an honest profession, they could do well.

It was now time for this thief to come to terms with his transgressions.

"Right," Jon answered. "When do we move in?"

There was silence on the other end of the line. "Nile?"

"Sorry, Jon, repeat your last statement."

"I said, 'when do we get this guy?'"

"Stand by. I'm being told that we need to catch what's his name..."

"His avatar is 'Byterunner'; his legal name is Taris Prilla."

"Right, we need to catch Mr. Byterunner in the act of stealing data for the arrest warrant to be valid."

Jon muttered under his breath. Byterunner didn't seem to adhere to any set schedule for his thefts. Sometimes he would stay off the data links for days at a time. They could be here a while.

Gryphon said, "Don't worry; your shift is over in another twelve hours."

Jon grimaced again, and wiped more water off his forehead. "What else does Infrared show? Weapons? Explosives?"

"Nothing but tamper-proof magnets inside his hard drives," Gryphon answered. "This won't be like last time."

"Glad to hear it," Jon said. "I just wish that..." He was interrupted by a ping from his equipment. "Hold on, I think our boy may be getting ready to go to work."

Jon's scanning equipment, interfaced directly to the power/comm mains running into the building, showed an incoming message to Byterunner's mailbox and an automatic reply being sent back out.

"Nile, is Byterunner moving around now?"

"Stand by," Several seconds passed as Jon waited, helplessly scanning the encrypted message. All that he could tell about the message was its origin and destination. Data thieves almost always used the strongest commercially-available encryption. Even with the computing resources at his disposal, Jon knew that he couldn't hope to glean enough meaningful information to be useful in the time he had. Maybe if he had a few dozen supercomputers and a decade...

Jon's pulse quickened. "OK, this may be it. Byterunner is interfacing to the public network, checking his messages. Seems like a lot of data traffic. OK, here goes several messages to the same network address. Checking the address – it's a bank."

Gryphon switched to the team channel. "OK, people this is it. Prospero, Thoms, you two have the side exit. Phipps, take your team through the back on my mark, and my team will take the front entrance. Prospero, status?"

Jon glanced up at his exit, then back down at the scanners. "He's still trying to hack into the bank. The attempts are methodical. I think he might be at this for several more minutes before he bails on this one and tries another."

The rain was now coming down in sheets.

Gryphon made the decision. "OK, let's do this. Two minutes to get in position. Go."

Jon unplugged his equipment from the power/comm mains, replaced the conduit cover, put on his tactical mask, and ran in a half-crouch toward his assigned exit. Jools Thoms was already there – they exchanged ready signs as they took their positions on either side of the exit.

Gryphon's voice was clipped and precise. "Set? Check? Go!"

Simultaneously, the access team silently flash-opened the front, back, and side doors, threw in disablement grenades, and the stakeout teams rushed in to the apartment.

Jon found the data thief in his bedroom, coughing and temporarily blinded by the grenades.

He was frantically trying to put on a black market tactical mask.

Jon quickly scanned the room for additional hazards: Byterunner wore a bulky vest with wires protruding out the sides. He quickly motioned Thoms to move back into the hallway and sent the entire team a visual of the scene. On the team channel he requested analysis and threat evaluation.

Jon called out, "Taris Prilla, you are under arrest. Stand still and put your hands above your head. Now!"

By now, Taris Prilla had gotten the mask on, and managed to answer in a choking voice, "Stay back, I'm wearing a suicide jacket, and I'll blow it!"

Jon backed up a step, but remained in the room. He could see tears streaming from Prilla's eyes. "Don't do anything foolish."

Recovering slightly, Taris Prilla laughed harshly. "I think that die has been cast, Government man. Back off or..."

Jon evaluated the rest of the room. The infrared scan hadn't revealed any additional explosives; he double-checked there were none.

Turning down the volume on his mask amplifier, Jon said calmly, "Now, let's take this one step at a time."

Blinking back stinging tears, Taris Prilla put one hand inside the jacket. "No, no, no, you're not going to take me. I'd rather die than disappear."

Jon paused. *That was an odd statement.* He said in his most reassuring voice, "Now calm down, nobody's going to disappear. Just take off your jacket, and put your hands on your head."

"Liar!" Taris Prilla choked.

Jon's internal comm chirped. Gryphon's voice was soft and steady. "Jon, we've analyzed the jacket.

It looks like the real thing, but we're confident it's a fake. This guy is desperate. We've scanned no other weapons or explosives. Take him down, and let's go home."

Jon moved forward and spread his hands in a conciliatory gesture, "OK, Taris, nobody's going to hurt you, but you'll have to come with us."

Realizing that Jon had guessed or been told that his jacket was harmless, the data thief jumped onto his bed and scrambled toward a window. Moving quickly, Jon grabbed the much smaller man, and pinned his arms behind him. Thoms and the rest of the team swarmed into the room, and began securing the equipment that overflowed from cabinets and desks.

While Jon held the man, Thoms quickly patted him down and retrieved several data crystals.

Jon couldn't help but notice that the thief was shaking with fear. For some reason, he felt an urge to comfort the man.

After he read Taris Prilla his rights as a citizen, he said, "Listen, it'll be all right. You've got to pay your debt to the citizenry, but then you'll have your life back."

Taris Prilla looked at him for an uncomfortably long time.

"You don't know, do you? I know. I hear things, I read things. People are disappearing. Not just people like me, either. Open your eyes."

Gryphon walked into the room. "OK, Mr. Prilla, do you have a statement to make. No? Let's get going then."

As he was led from the apartment, Taris Prilla called back to Jon, "Open your eyes – before it's too late."

Down is Out

Gryphon and Taris Prilla, the data thief known as Byterunner, got into a police transport and drove off into the rain-soaked night.

Chapter 2

Jon got home just as the rain was ending. Standing in a puddle in the foyer, he removed his standard-issue and wholly-inadequate raincoat. The apartment was silent, but he noticed a wonderful aroma coming from the kitchen. He followed his nose and found a plate of cinnamon-blueberry muffins and a note taped to the microwave: "For post-stakeout appetites. Heat for 30 seconds. Love, Lara."

He heated the muffins and got some milk from the refrigerator. Sitting at the kitchen table, with the steaming muffins and cold milk in front of him, he realized just how tired, cold, and hungry he had been. He wolfed down the muffins, drank the milk, and put the dishes in the sink.

Feeling much better, he walked softly up the stairs to the bedroom. Lara was sleeping on her side, and stirred when he sat down on his side of the bed.

"Morning. Is everything all right?" she said sleepily.

"Shhh, yes, go back to sleep. I love you."

"I love you mmmm."

He went to the bathroom, took a hot shower, and then lay down beside his sleeping wife. He was asleep as soon as his head hit his pillow.

When Jon awoke, Lara had already left for work. He stretched lazily, luxuriating in the warmth of the flannel sheets. Reluctantly, he got out of bed, took another hot shower and shaved.

For breakfast, Lara had left him breakfast wraps beside the microwave. This time, instead of a handwritten note, she had left him an ImageNote. He picked up the small device and placed it on the kitchen table. He pressed a button on the side of the device, and a three-dimensional image of his wife appeared beside the table.

As he bit into the delectable concoction of scrambled eggs, sausage, cheese, onion, and hot peppers, the image of Lara said, "Honey, I'm sorry we missed each other this morning, but I assume since you were in early, your assignment was completed, so that's a good thing. Now, you get a few normal workdays before your next assignment, right? I hope so."

"If it's all right with you, I've invited some friends over tomorrow night – nothing special, just a potluck dinner and an advance screening of an independent movie. You remember my friend Oma? She's spent the last year writing and directing this project, and I can't wait to see it. I think you'll like it too. It's about the good old days in the Outer Territories. I'll see you when I get home tonight. Love you."

She blew him a kiss, and the image faded.

He finished his breakfast, put on his coat, and walked down to the tram.

The day was bright and windy, with dead leaves pasted to the streets by last night's storm. He hugged

9

himself as an unusually strong gust showered him with more dead leaves from the big oak trees lining his street.

At this time of the morning, the tram stop was relatively empty, and he grabbed a seat all by himself in the back of the tram. *I should come into work late more often*, he thought. After he got on, a young girl and two older men got on and sat down several rows in front of him.

He sat back as the tram pulled away from the stop and accelerated toward the center city, passing several abandoned construction projects.

In the past several years, the planetary economy had dipped into a mild depression, which always increased the crime rate. The current Imperium Council of Overseers had recently pledged a new program of economic growth. 'Prosperity was just around the corner', the politicians said. He would wait and see. Both he and Lara were lucky to be workers in different branches of the Imperium. His branch, the Imperium Civil Stability Group, was responsible for maintaining public order, enforcing the laws of the lands, and coordinating with other groups on matters relating to civil stability. Lara worked directly for the Imperium Council of Overseers as an advocate and legal analyst.

The Council of Overseers served as the elected representative body of the people. The Council was composed of the directors of all the major Imperium groups: In addition to Civil Stability, there was the Infrastructure group – responsible for power, water, waste disposal, communications, and transportation; the Mercantile group – responsible for regulating and maintaining commerce; and the LifeQuality group – responsible for health care, recreation, and education.

The tram arrived at the Civil Stability group complex of buildings. Jon got off and walked briskly to his building and took the lift to his floor.

He looked forward to an easy day – paperwork for the raid last night, check in with some people, and maybe even leave a little early.

He spent the next few hours finishing his final report of the Byterunner raid, pausing now and then to answer a few routine requests and questions.

By lunchtime, he was ready to get out of the office for awhile. He walked down to the tram stop, and jumped on the first downtown tram that came by. He felt good – it was always a good feeling to finish an assignment – especially one that ended successfully and safely.

But something was nagging him. Maybe it was the suspect's intensity when he insisted that he would rather die than be taken into custody. But it was lunchtime now, and if there was one thing he had learned in his years working in Civil Stability – you learned not to take your problems home or to lunch – they'll always be at your desk when you get back.

He got off the tram at the city center mall – the scenic heart of the city, with a backdrop of the majestic spires of the Imperium Council Chambers reaching up to the sky, and a colorful bazaar of shops, museums, cafes, and food vending stalls all around the mall. Even on cold and rainy days, there was life and vitality here.

He strolled by some clothing vendors, idly searching for a pretty scarf to buy for Lara. Not finding anything that really caught his eye, he stopped by a pastry vendor, and got a spiced meat pastry for lunch, then walked leisurely down to the central reflecting pool.

As he sat down by the side of the pool, his comm chirped. It was his partner Syd Shining. They had recently been assigned to different projects, and hadn't spoken for several weeks.

"Syd, how are you, partner?"

Syd's voice was barely audible, and strangely distorted, as if he were broadcasting on an extremely low-power channel.

"Syd, I can barely hear you."

"I know," replied Syd. "Listen, I don't have long, but I wanted to check in. Have you noticed anything....strange....lately?"

"What do you mean by strange?"

"I mean anyone saying weird stuff about people disappearing..."

Jon instantly recalled the fear in Taris Prilla's eyes.

"Yeah, last night as a matter of fact. Hey, where are you?"

The signal was growing fainter. "I'll tell you later. Also – and this is important – don't tell *anyone* that we talked. And I mean anyone – not Lara, especially not anyone back at the office, understand?"

"OK, fine. I hope this line isn't tapped, then." Jon joked.

"Trust me, it isn't."

"So what do you know about people disappearing?"

"I'm still gathering evidence, but I suspect so...." His voice was drowned out in a wave of static.

"Syd? Syd?"

"...signal is degrading. Listen, I'll be in touch. And remember, this call never happened."

Jon looked around the plaza. "Right. Syd... one more thing?"

But he was gone.

Jon stood up and casually but methodically scanned the plaza, looking for any tell-tales of eavesdroppers. Satisfied that no one had overheard him, he shrugged, tossed his pastry wrapper into a waste disposal bin and headed back toward the office.

When he got back to his work cube, he logged on to the Central repository and queried the subject of last night's raid – Taris Prilla. He expected to see a record of the arrest process, including his own account of the raid, submitted that morning. Instead, the message '**No such person on file – Taris Prilla**' appeared on his screen.

Puzzled, he tried the search again, using several different spellings for Prilla. None of the searches found Prilla's record. He even tried using Prilla's pseudonym Byterunner. Still nothing.

Scowling at the message on the screen, Jon placed a call to Data Repository Support – maybe something was wrong with the system.

The smart software that answered his call was calm, friendly, and professional. Jon hated it.

"How may I assist you today, Mr. Prospero?"

"I, uh, I'm having trouble locating a record I created this morning. Can you help me find it?"

"Of course, I will do my best. Please state the full name of the subject."

"Taris Prilla, aka Byterunner. Apprehended this morning at about two hundred hours."

"When was the report filed please?"

"This morning."

"Please wait while I locate that record."

Annoyingly upbeat music began playing as Jon waited for a response. With all the musical styles in existence today, why did the company pick the one style that nobody liked?

Several minutes later, the voice said, "I'm sorry, but there is no 'Taris Prilla, aka Byterunner' in any existing Data Repository."

Jon stared at his screen. "But that's impossible. I updated the record myself with information about last night's, I mean, this morning's arrest."

He thought a moment, then asked, "Are all repositories available?"

He thought he heard a trace of haughtiness when the voice immediately responded, "Yes, all Imperium Data Repositories are available and online. No problems, failures, or anomalies have been recorded in the last three hundred forty six standard..."

"OK, ok. Is there an escalation procedure for reporting missing data?"

This time, he was sure he detected haughtiness. "Any anomalies, perceived or real, must be submitted by your supervisor, who is..."

After the slightest pause, the voice finished, "Stafal Frimm. Would you like me to connect you to his office?"

"No thank you. I'll go see him myself."

"Thank you for calling Data Repository Support. Have a nice day."

Jon sat back in his chair, feeling a little dizzy. What did all this mean?

On a whim, he tried to search for his last three arrests. The computer had no record of any of them. Now he desperately wanted to talk to Syd. What was going on?

He hesitated for a moment, then called Nile Gryphon.

"Nile, have you done the paperwork on last night's case?"

Nile answered, "Of course, I did it this morning. Why do you ask?"

Jon said. "It's funny, I went back to the record to check some things, and the record I entered is gone."

Nile's voice grew stern. "You re-opened your own file? You know you're not supposed to do that."

Trying to sound contrite, Jon said, "I know, but something with that case just didn't sit right. Can you, as a favor, trying calling up some of your recent cases?"

Nile said, "Sorry. No can do. I'm on a glide path to retirement, and I don't want to do anything, anything to mess that up. You never know who's watching what. And as a favor to you, young man, I didn't hear what you just said."

Jon grinned. "OK. Thanks anyway."

As he closed the connection, Jon decided to head home for the day, when his screen chimed, and displayed Stafal Frimm's sallow face.

"Jon, do you have a minute? Come on up." The screen went blank.

Jon sighed and made his way to Frimm's office.

Chapter 3

Stafal Frimm had been Jon's supervisor for the past five years, and Jon had found him a constant irritation. A perfect example of the upwardly mobile bureaucrat, Stafal was a magician at the art of self-promotion. To Jon's knowledge, Stafal had never had an original idea, had never lead anything, had never organized anything, had really never written any reports, had never analyzed anything; he had just taken credit for the hard work and sacrifices of others. It was an enduring mystery to Jon why his superiors didn't see what a phony Stafal was.

Stafal's office was a sumptuous suite overlooking the riverpark. Big desk, the newest, fastest, most expensive computers (unused, Jon thought sourly), even a private washroom.

Jon stood in the open doorway and knocked on the door.

Stafal sat at his desk staring at a thick report, brows knit in concentration.

Trying to keep his annoyance in check, Jon knocked again.

After a lengthy pause, Stafal looked up and said, "Oh, Jon, come on in. Take a seat."

Jon walked up to one of three smaller chairs in front of Stafal's desk and sat down.

"Sorry, I'll be with you in a minute – just catching up on some quarterly statistics."

Jon waited as Stafal pretended to scan the voluminous documents, occasionally muttering 'Interesting', or 'We'll need to follow up on this.'

Just as Jon was about to concoct an emergency so he could leave this very unpleasant man's office, Stafal closed the report he had been 'working on' and steepled his fingers in front of him.

Jon said nothing. Stafal looked at Jon with a furrowed brow and said, "Jon, I'll get right to the point."

He paused, and Jon waited. *I'd really like to punch this guy in the nose,* he thought. Despite himself, he smiled slightly.

Not noticing Jon's smile, Stafal leaned back in his chair.

"I've been getting some odd reports about some data requests you've made."

Jon said calmly, "Really? How so? I was going to talk to you about the same thing."

Not giving any indication that he had heard Jon, Stafal continued, "It seems that you've been 'following up' on some arrests that you've made in recent weeks and months. Now I'm sure that you know as well as I that such requests properly belong to the Post capture group – that's their job, after all."

"Yes, I know, but I thought that…"

"And you know that the group cannot allow such requests to come from unauthorized sources. We simply don't have the resources."

"But they were my reports…" Jon began.

Stafal tone grew sterner. "You are well aware that it is every person's duty to optimize departmental resources."

Jon decided to follow the path of least resistance. "Yes sir."

"I'll have to dock you a vacation day for this, you understand."

Jon gritted his teeth and said, "Yes sir."

Smiling now (the sadist), Stafal cooed, "I'm sure we won't let that happen again, will we?"

Briefly wondering just how much trouble he'd be in if he just punched Stafal out right now, Jon thought of Lara, swallowed, and said meekly, "No."

"Good, otherwise your performance has been..." He consulted another chart on his desk, "acceptable."

"Thank you sir."

Jon wondered if the interview was now over. Stafal examined his manicured hands and asked, "Oh, by the way, have you spoken to your partner, um, Syd Shining, recently?"

Jon remembered their conversation and Syd's plea for silence. He said smoothly, "I spoke to him briefly before his last assignment, but that was over a month ago."

Stafal was looking at him closely now. "Oh really? I would think that longtime partners would keep in better touch."

Jon looked at him steadily.

"I was busy on my last assignment. I assumed that Syd was also heads down. For all I know, he could have a deep cover assignment. I'm well aware of the department rules concerning deep cover." Jon said seriously. *Take that, you noodle*, he thought.

Stafal was frowning now. "Are you sure you haven't talked to him? The reason I ask is that we seem to," he cleared his throat, "have lost touch with him."

Mustering what he hoped was the right amount of innocent concern, Jon said, "Lost touch? Is there anything I can do to assist? I'll gladly redistribute my workload and..."

Stafal snapped, "No, that won't be necessary. Return to your duties." He waved a hand dismissively.

Jon stood up. "Thank you sir."

As Jon walked out of the office, Stafal called after him, "One more thing." Jon stopped and faced Stafal.

"If you do hear from your partner, you will report to me immediately. Is that clear?"

Jon said, "Absolutely clear."

———————

On the way home, Jon tried to connect the dots. The whole day (beginning with last night's stakeout and raid) had taken on the aspect of a not-very-good vid-drama – disjointed, with too many loose ends. What he needed was a run, some dinner, and a good night's sleep.

When he arrived home, the apartment was dark. He ordered the house lights to come on, but the house system didn't seem to be functioning either. He unhooked a lightwand from his card ring, and went in search for the access control panel. As he was moving some boxes in the utility room to get to the panel, he thought, *When did we get so much junk? Is all this Lara's?*

When he finally got the panel open, everything looked in order, including the battery backup. Very strange.

He called the building's support computer to place a power restore order, but, to his surprise, the computer relayed him to a human being, who seemed equally surprised to be talking to a real, live customer.

"Hello, my name is Jon Prospero, and I'm calling to report a power outage?"

"Have you checked your access control panel?" the technician asked.

"Yeah, looks OK to me." Jon answered.

"OK, let me patch in to that grid and take a look."

Jon waited. At least the power company didn't provide annoying music.

After a few minutes, the technician came back on the line.

"Mr. Prospero? Our records show that you were disconnected for non-payment. But this is odd, usually we disconnect at the beginning of the month, and this was done just an hour ago. Let me check with Accounting. Would you like to hear some music while you wait?"

"No thanks," Jon said quickly.

"Hmm, not a music lover," said the technician. "I'll be back in a few minutes. Thanks for waiting."

Jon decided to turn off his lightwand to save the battery and sat down on the floor in the dark.

A few minutes later he heard the front door open and close, and then Lara's voice.

He got up and turned the lightwand back on to guide her to him.

"What happened to the lights?" she asked.

"I'm working on that right now."

She looked at the boxes stacked beside the panel. "When did we get so much junk? Is this stuff yours?" she asked.

They sat down on the floor and Jon turned the lightwand off again.

"Jon, we're sitting in the dark."

Jon said, "I'm trying to save the battery."

"Don't we have another lightwand?"

"I want to save that one too. You never know."

Lara said, "Tough day?"

Jon said, "It was OK."

"'OK', like a normal workday, or 'OK' like you don't want to talk about it," she persisted.

"It was fine, how was yours?"

Lara sat back on some unfolded clothes, and said, "Same old, same old. Diplomatic conferences, trade treaties, security treaties. Millions in revenue at stake, thousands of jobs, and all these people can think about is who is sitting across from whom, and what kind of flavored water is being served."

Since Lara had come in, Jon had completely forgotten about the call to the power company, so when the technical came back on the line, they both jumped.

"Sorry to keep you waiting. Accounting does confirm that you were disconnected for non-payment, but they also have a record of your payment for this month's debit on another system, so we'll restore your power while we investigate this further."

The lights all over the house came on.

"Sorry for the trouble."

Jon got to his feet and helped Lara up. He said, "Thanks for your help. No trouble. It was kind of nice." He smiled at his wife.

The technician said, "Hey, thanks for not yelling at me. Have a good night. End call."

As they walked to the kitchen, Lara said, "You still haven't told me about your day."

Jon sat down at the kitchen table. "It was fine", he said, a little testily this time.

She came over and hugged him from behind. "That bad, huh?"

His comm unit chirped. "Got a call," he said,"

Lara frowned and let go. "Oh, for goodness sakes. If it's work, tell them you're off duty." She left the room.

"Prospero here, go ahead."

"Jon, it's me."

"Syd, man, I need to talk to you," Jon whispered urgently. "I've had the most bizarre afternoon. Where are you?"

"Ask me no questions..."

"OK, fine. By the way, Stafal Frimm is looking for you."

Syd chuckled. "I bet he is. Did he call you to his office?"

Wincing at the memory, Jon said, "Yeah, it was big fun. I don't think he believed me when I told him I hadn't heard from you."

"Don't worry, he looks like that all the time. Listen, I can't guarantee the security of this line much longer, so I want you to meet me at the Fourth Circle Water Purification Facility tomorrow at quarter to twelve, sharp. Be there."

"Hey, that's a pretty big place, where will you be?"

"Just follow the sound of falling water. I'll find you."

"And Jon?"

"Yeah?"

"Don't talk to Lara about this; don't talk to anyone about this until I see you. OK?"

"Right."

"One last thing."

"What?"

"Assume that you will be followed to the meeting, so make sure you lose that person before you arrive. Got it?"

"Check. I'll be there. Alone."

"Until then, take care."

"You too."

Lara called from the bedroom, "Who was that?"

"Work," Jon answered.

The next day, Jon slipped out of the office a little after eleven. He took Syd's advice seriously and made sure anybody who tried to follow him would end up disappointed. He got on the northbound tram (away from the water plant) toward Circle Three, getting off at several stops on the way. He scrutinized the crowds flowing in and out of the trams at each stop to try and identify a stalker, and just for good measure, took a taxi to a park adjacent to the Circle Four Water Plant. He walked in through the public tour entrance, and stopped to admire the six-story tall waterfalls that stood like glistening dominos extending back through the plant. *Follow the falling water,* he said to himself, and began walking toward the last waterfall. The place was almost deserted, with only a handful of people walking around the waterfalls nearest the entrance. As he neared the last waterfall he looked at his watch – quarter to twelve exactly. There was nobody near this waterfall, except a maintenance worker wearing an orange jumpsuit – hold on, that was Syd!

He walked casually over to a nearby bench and sat down. Syd turned his back to him and began sweeping the walkway.

"Jon, don't look at me, just look up at the waterfall."

"Syd, why are we..."

"Listening devices can't filter out waterfall sounds. I'm taking no chances."

Obediently, Jon looked up at the coruscating sheets of water. "Syd, are you all right?"

Sweep, sweep. "That's a relative question. I may have stumbled upon something that very well could get me killed. I considered not telling you – to protect you."

"Hey, we're partners – if you're in trouble..."

"Those stories about people disappearing – they're not stories; people are disappearing. And I think I know where they go."

Despite himself, Jon looked at Syd's back. "You do?"

"There's a secret prison somewhere – that's where they send them."

"Who are 'they'?"

"The Civil Stability Group. Maybe the Overseers know, too. I haven't been able to confirm that, though. Medusa Mercantus is definitely behind it all."

"The group leader? Stafal's boss? But why?"

"Think about it. How much easier maintaining stability becomes if the troublemakers, the dissidents, the freethinkers just disappear."

"This is bad."

"Oh yeah."

It's a conspiracy, then," Jon said.

Now it was Syd's turn to look up.

"What?"

"Yesterday, I tried to look up several of my arrest records. They were gone."

Syd swept faster. "Jon, you shouldn't have done that."

"Oh, yeah. That's why I was in Stafal's office. He took away a vacation day."

Syd swept up a pile of debris and got out a vacuum. "Jon, I think you should get Lara out of town for awhile. This could get ugly."

Two men in orange jumpsuits slowly made their way toward Jon and Syd. Jon had been staring at the falling water most of the time, but Syd noticed the two and moved closer to Jon.

"Heads up. We've got company – those two work for Medusa Mercantus."

"Are you sure?"

"Water plant workers don't usually carry automatic weapons."

The two undercover security agents moved steadily toward Jon and Syd.

"OK, what do we do now?"

"Run!"

Jon ducked behind a concrete bench as a shot rammed into the sidewall, showering him with concrete chips and dust. Another shot went wide and pinged in the waterfall, blowing a chunk of concrete support into the water.

Syd sprinted toward a maintenance chamber behind the last waterfall, slamming the door shut seconds before one of the agents fired two grenades at the chamber. An instant later, the door of the chamber blew inward. Fire and smoke billowed out of the open doorway.

Jon jumped over the railing into the water, hoping for some cover. He looked up toward the support and saw a door. Diving quickly to the bottom of the pool, he swam underneath the waterfall up into a small maintenance chamber below the main support.

Breathing heavily, he called Lara at work.

After a few moments, she answered, "Honey, what is it?"

"Shhh," he hissed. "Listen carefully, I don't have much time. Leave work right now, but don't go home. Get away from the city."

"But..." she began.

"Listen. Somebody, somebody who works for Medusa Mercantus is trying to kill me. I think they just killed Syd, too."

"What? But why?"

"People are disappearing, there's a prison... I don't have time. You have to get away. Now."

Just above him, too close, Jon heard voices, then splashes.

"Lara, I love you. I have to go."

"Jon, I love you too. When..."

"Honey, go!" He cut the connection.

Frantically, Jon looked for a way out. He climbed up to a grating at the top of the chamber and opened it. He wriggled through to find himself inside the main support for the waterfall. He started climbing and gradually worked his way higher and higher into the structure. He looked out through the holes in the support at one of the men standing below him. The man raised his gun and fired. He felt a sharp sting in his arm, then his vision blurred and his entire body began to go cold. He fell into water and darkness.

———— —— ——

Painful, bright light. A soft voice.

"Mr. Prospero?"

A very ungentle slap across his face. The same voice, this time not so soft.

"Mr. Prospero, wake up. We need to talk."

He struggled to open his eyes. He was lying on a cold metal table in some kind of storage area. Out of the corner of his eye he could see shelves full of gray boxes and red cylinders.

He tried to lift his head, but couldn't.

"Jon, take it easy. You've had a busy day." He knew that voice – Stafal Frimm.

"Where am I?" Jon managed to croak.

"Somewhere we won't be disturbed," said Stafal Frimm. "How are you feeling?"

"I want to see a lawyer," said Jon with as much force as he could muster.

"Oh, I don't think so", said the velvety soft voice of Medusa Mercantus, group leader of the Imperium Civil Stability group.

Frimm continued, "Jon, Jon, you've been a bad boy, meeting with criminals and not telling us."

"What are you talking about?" Jon asked weakly.

"Oh, I think you know. Your former partner, Syd Shining, has turned rogue, and you were caught talking to him. Not a good thing at all, I'm afraid." He smiled unpleasantly.

Jon's vision cleared, and he was able to move his head a little.

They were probably in one of the sub-basements of one of the Civil Stability buildings. Beside himself, Stafal Frimm, and Medusa Mercantus, four large guards stood at each corner of the room. Each held a menacingly large pulse rifle.

"I don't know anything." Before he could react, Medusa lashed out and struck him on the face, much harder this time. He tasted blood.

"Do not play us for fools, Mr. Prospero. You are familiar with carrot and stick interrogation techniques, I believe?"

"Stick." She struck him again, hard.

"Carrot. If you cooperate with us, we can guarantee the liberty and safety of your wife. We have apprehended her at her office in the Gardens building, and are holding her now."

In the Gardens building? Jon thought. Lara had just moved into a new office in another building last week. She had complained just yesterday that the Personnel Repository was still delivering her mail to her old office. *So they didn't have her!*

Mustering up his best defensive attitude, he said, "You know that holding an innocent family member in an investigation is against the law."

Bending over him, and placing her cold hand against his cheek, Medusa said, "You know, I'll just have to look that one up."

She gripped his jaw and stared into his eyes. "Tell me about your conversation with Mr. Shining. Be complete and truthful and..." She looked at Frimm.

Frimm looked momentarily panicked.

"His wife's name?" she hissed.

"Lara," he said quickly.

"And Lara will be just fine. Lie to me and...well let's just say that you wouldn't want to be responsible for your wife's suffering, now would you?"

"You wouldn't dare."

"Oh, I have, I do, and I will."

Getting feeling back in his arms and legs, Jon estimated his chances with the guards. *If he could grab Medusa and use her as a shield...*

Stafal pushed his head back down. "Don't even think about what you're thinking about now. Your best option is to lie back, relax and tell us what we want to know."

Gambling on more time, Jon decided to tell them. After all, Syd was dead, and if what he had told Jon were true, he wouldn't be telling them anything they didn't already know.

"All right, but you have to promise that Lara will be released completely unharmed. If I find out that she has in any way been mistreated..."

"Of course," Medusa cooed. "One of the guards will take care of that now."

She glared at the guard closest to the door, and snapped, "Go!"

Momentarily confused, the guard obeyed at once.

"Right." Jon said. "I need to get in a more comfortable position."

Stafal Frimm said, "You're lying down, that's the most comfortable position."

"Don't play games now," Medusa threatened.

"All right," Jon said. "Syd wanted to meet with me to tell me that he had found some sort of prison that had been specially built to house dissidents and political prisoners."

Medusa and Stafal looked at each other.

She asked, "And did he give you the location of this prison?"

"No, your people blew him up before he could tell me."

The guard came back in and whispered something to her. Her face twisted into a scowl and she slapped him again.

"Where is your wife?"

"You said you had her. You promised she would be released."

"I was misinformed." She glared at Stafal Frimm, who blanched.

"Where is she?" Medusa demanded.

"I don't know," Jon said.

Visibly angry now, Medusa Mercantus leaned over him and said, "Well, I can promise you this, former Investigator Jon Prospero of the Imperium Civil Stability Group, when we do catch your wife, I'll make a recording of her interrogation and make you watch it."

She straightened up.

"Also, since you seem to be so eager to find out more about this so-called prison, I've arranged for a visit."

Blackness, coolness. Floating. Jon was in the Imperium courtyard. It was around dusk, only some of the vendors were still doing business. He smelled the sharp, pungent smell of roasting nuts. Was he supposed to meet someone here? He couldn't remember. What day was today? He had the sensation that he was forgetting something very important, something urgent, but what? He walked over to a hot drink vendor, and was about to buy something when he saw Lara across the courtyard waving to him. He started walking toward her. She was saying something, but he was too far away to hear. As he got closer, he could just barely hear her, but she wasn't talking, she was humming. A low hum.

The hum of fluorescent light.

He felt someone touch his arm. Instinctively he grabbed the arm and flipped the man onto his back, pinning him down.

"Take it easy," the man said in a strangled voice. "No harm intended."

"Sorry," Jon said, and released the man. He got to his feet unsteadily and staggered to a wall.

He was in a rectangular room, perhaps large enough to hold ten people without crowding. In addition to the man who had awakened him, two women watched him warily. One, very attractive, was a bit taller than Jon. She had brown hair, looked physically fit, and was probably his age or a bit older. The younger woman, who looked like she was going to cry, was the shortest of them all, and had short blond hair.

They were all dressed in rough, brown coveralls with no pockets.

"Who are you?" Jon said roughly.

The man, shorter than Jon, but more muscular, extended his hand tentatively.

"I'm Tem Koltoo, and this," he indicated the older woman, "is Kiala Cmeeli, and this," he indicated the younger woman, "is Jona Altsul."

Both women nodded as they were introduced.

"Jon Prospero." He shook Tem's offered hand. "Sorry again about the wrestling move. Reflex. I hope you've had a better day that I have."

Jona laughed bitterly. "We seem to have ended up in the same place."

"Which is where exactly?" Jon asked. "How long have you all been here?"

Kiala said, "I got here first, probably several hours ago. Tem fell through that opening maybe an hour after I woke up, and Jona maybe a few hours afterward."

"As to the question of where we are, I don't know. Someone's idea of a very bad prank."

Tem said, "I have a theory."

Jona snorted, and walked away toward the far side of the room.

Lowering his voice, Tem said, "She's apparently not much into theories."

Jon said, "OK. What theory?"

Tem said, "I'm a graduate student, working on an advanced degree in civil planning, and for the past several months, I've been doing research on population count anomalies in random communities – you know census glitches, that kind of stuff.

"I've been doing some field research, and I started hearing about these, well, urban legends. People disappearing in the night, leaving no trace whatsoever in the morning, authorities know nothing – really bizarre stuff. In the course of my research, I heard this so often that I considered changing my topic to urban folklore. The descriptions were all amazingly consistent.

"I gathered up my research, and submitted my preliminary findings. A few days later, I got called into the department chair's office, and was told to stop my research. Just like that.

"Well, one of my friends worked at a public data repository, and I got her to check on some of the names that people had given me, and there were no repository records on them. Nothing. So either there was this incredible, coordinated hoax aimed just at me, or people really were vanishing into thin air."

"Or being sent here," Jon said.

"Where is here?" asked Kiala.

"Apparently it's a prison for people like us." Jon said, and sat down heavily against the wall.

"What do you mean, 'people like us?'" asked Jona.

"I don't know – people on the verge of finding out about this place," Jon guessed.

Jona nodded and asked Jon, "Why are you here?"

"I'm an Investigator with Civil Stability," Jon said.

Jona stiffened.

"My partner found out about this place." Jon continued. "He told me that much, then was killed before he could tell me any more. But it was enough for Medusa Mercantus to send me here."

Kiala clapped her hands together once. "Now I know why I'm here then."

"I'm an auditor for the Imperium General Accounting group and I had just begun doing an audit of Civil Stability."

"Oh boy," said Jon.

"Oh boy is right," said Kiala. "The scant documentation I was given to start was enough to trigger a full-scale group audit, but when I presented evidence that the Civil Stability leadership was not cooperating – actually they were downright threatening – my superiors, who are normally not people who can be intimidated, let me tell you, quietly took me aside and told me to call off my investigation.

"By this time, I had managed to find proof positive that group leader Mercantus had been siphoning off funds from other Civil Stability projects. When I presented this evidence to my boss, he asked me if the copy in his hands was the only copy. I said of course not, we archive everything. He thanked me, and told me I had done a good job in a voice that said I had definitely not done a good job, and that I should take the afternoon off."

"I had been working pretty hard lately, so I grabbed a quick lunch, and came home for a nap. The next thing I know, I'm lying on the floor in this room."

Jon frowned. "The long arm of the law."

He looked at Jona, "So, why do you think you're here?"

She glared at Jon as she answered, "I'm a data thief."

"I was doing a job for a client, breaking into one of the more specialized repositories, and I came across this cache of deleted names. I recognized some of the names, artsy types, and started poking around the cache. I anonymously accessed a public data store, and cross-checked some of the names – *they weren't there*, and I know at least one of the people on the list, 'cause I stole some money from his account a few months ago."

"I must have stayed hooked up too long in the first repository, 'cause one of your sniffers caught me. A freelancer like myself has to live by her wits, and I just couldn't deal with the resources of the Civil Stability group. It wasn't a fair fight."

"It's not supposed to be," Jon said. Jona snorted and turned away.

Kiala looked up at the featureless ceiling and asked, "I wonder how much longer we'll have to stay in here."

Tem shrugged. "If half of what I've heard is true, we should be lucky to stay in here. Our 'hosts' are going to do with us what they will in their own time. I'm going to lie down."

Jon said, "Maybe it is a good idea to rest."

Down is Out

He sat down against the wall and closed his eyes.

——— —— ——

Standing in the Imperium Plaza again. This time, it was snowing – huge, beautiful flakes drifting down out of a cotton candy sky. He scraped the ground with his boot, making a small arc-shaped snowdrift. He felt again as if there was something he had forgotten – gloves, scarf? He looked down at his feet again, and now he was wearing skates, and was skating effortlessly around the plaza. He stopped to look around, then noticed he was moving forward again, downhill, faster and faster...

——— —— ——

He awoke when he bumped in to Kiala.

"What's happening?"

The floor was slanting farther and farther downward.

"You tell me," said Tem.

The floor was now at an angle that made it impossible to stand up.

"Pretty soon, we'll be sitting on the wall," said Kiala.

"I don't think so," said Jona, as the wall opened and the four prisoners tumbled through.

Chapter 4

They found themselves in a vast chamber many times larger than the one they had just occupied. Jon looked around and saw thousands of other prisoners, all wearing the same drab outfits, all looking angry or frightened or confused. Two giant viewscreens occupied opposing walls.

There were no doors, windows, or ventilation grills that Jon could see, but he had a feeling that they were now deep underground.

Robots stood guard around the chamber. Each robot was slightly taller than an average man, and held what looked like a blunt club – no doubt to be used for crowd control if necessary. In any event, it was very useful as a symbol. Jon noted that no one dared to approach them for a closer look.

The viewscreens sputtered with static, then resolved to an image of a man.

"I am Derin Thanatos, your Overwarden. I welcome you, and I'm going to explain some things to you that will make your stay with us more pleasant."

"Is this guy for real?" whispered Tem to Jon.

"Don't know, he acts a lot like my ex-boss," whispered Jon back.

"This place is not a place of torment," boomed the Overwarden's voice, "but a place of repentance. If you work well and long, you will absolve yourself of the error that brought you here. Work will make you free."

Boos and catcalls rang out from the crowd.

Kiala whispered, "Does he think we're buying any of this?"

Jon whispered back, "It won't hurt to listen to what he says. Do you get the feeling that we're no longer on the surface?"

She looked around and wrinkled her nose. "Yeah, I think that's right. There's something...oppressive... about this room."

Jon snorted, and Kiala quickly added, "Well, more oppressive than your normal prison courtyard would be."

Jon looked at her and said, "How would you know?"

She looked back up at the Overwarden. "Shut up, I want to listen to this."

While they were talking, an automaton approached them, club raised. When it was several feet away, it said in a fluid mechanical voice, "You will be quiet while the Overwarden is talking."

Jon thought it prudent to not answer, so he turned, winking at Kiala, and faced the screen again. The robot returned to its post.

The Overwarden's image now filled the viewscreen. He must have intended this to make him seem more imposing, but Jon thought it just made him look cartoonish.

"The fundamental rule of this facility is discipline. Obey the rules, and work hard, and you will be well treated. Disobey the rules, and you will be dealt with according to the infraction."

Tem whispered, "I wonder if he's going to take questions at the end."

"Shut up," said Jona.

"Each group of you will be looked after by your Section Wardens. Each Section Warden is answerable only to me.

"You will receive further instruction about prison rules in the coming days. Remember what I said earlier. You are all here because you have violated Imperium law and have been found to be dangerous to the stability of our great Society. In here, you can work for relief, you can work for forgiveness, you can work to better the lives of those people you would have otherwise harmed."

His voice grew louder. "Obey your wardens."

His image disappeared and the chamber grew noticeably darker.

"Do any of you feel sleepy?" asked Jon. He guessed that they had pumped in some kind of pacification gas through the ventilation system.

Jona said, "Yeah, and a little weak-kneed. Mr. Superwarden's speech must have gotten to me."

Tem guessed, "Pac-gas?"

Jon said, "Probably. They might also have mixed it with some kind of agent to make us more open to suggestion."

Kiala stumbled. "I really would just like to lie down for awhile."

Just then, Jon noticed that dozens of transparent bubbles descending from openings in the ceiling to the floor of the chamber. Each bubble gathered up a group of people.

Fighting his own fatigue, Jon studied the operation for several minutes and concluded that each bubble was picking up exactly five people – no more, no less – then rising to disappear into an opening in the ceiling.

"I assume that we want to stay together, at least for the short term?" Jon asked.

The others nodded.

"Then I'd suggest that we recruit one more member to our little party."

Tem had been watching too. "The bubbles are picking up five people, and there are four of us."

"Right, and I think it might be better if we chose who our new companion might be, rather than have the choice made for us."

Kiala said, "That sounds like a good idea. Who do we look for?"

By now, the bubbles had carried away a good quarter of the prisoners, and the remainder continued murmuring and milling around. There wasn't much of anything else to do.

"Somebody who's physically non-threatening, someone who doesn't look like he or she will go psychotic."

Jona laughed harshly. "Well, that rules out everybody here."

Tem pointed across the chamber to several people milling about a good distance from each other.

"What about her?" He pointed to a small dark-haired woman standing by herself.

Jon said, "She just looks afraid like the rest of us. I think it might be better if two of us ask her to join us. Tem and Kiala? If you both go, and Kiala does the asking, she might feel less afraid."

Tem and Kiala nodded.

Jon looked up at the ceiling. "Hurry – it looks like our turn is coming up."

They hurried across the chamber and approached the woman. Jon could see her reluctance to join them, but either Kiala or Tem must have been a good talker because eventually all three began walking back to Jon and Jona.

Jona looked up just as another bubble was descending from the ceiling.

"Hey Jon, tell them to get a move on. Look up."

By now, the bubble was clearly heading for them, slowly but steadily.

Jon waved his hands and shouted for the others to hurry up.

As the three ran up, the bubble descended on the group, and they all fell asleep inside it as it drifted up toward the ceiling.

Chapter 5

Jon woke with a bad taste in his mouth and a throbbing head. *This is getting old*, he thought.

He lay on a mat in a dimly lit rectangular cell. His companions, still sleeping, were sprawled on either side of him. There was a small basin in the corner and a toilet curtained off from the sleeping area. It wasn't much, but it was better than he had expected. An opening at the end of the cell was crisscrossed in a grid of light.

Outside the cell he saw thousands of similar cells lining the six walls of a enormous chamber. He couldn't see what level they were on, but they were closer to the high ceiling of the chamber that they were to the floor. Each wall was a different color. On the ground floor, at the intersection of each wall were what looked like access doorways, now closed. In the middle of the open area was a tall column covered with blunt, hollow spikes jutting out in all directions. Jon suspected they contained cameras or self-directing long-range guns – probably both.

Jon reached out to touch the grid, when a voice said from the back of the cell, "I wouldn't do that if I were you."

Jon whirled around to face the voice.

"Who are you?"

"Name's Deemus. Who are you?"

"Name's Jon. Why shouldn't I touch the grid?"

"'Lectrified. Give you a nasty shock. Try it if you want, but our Warden won't like it, nope."

"Why would the Warden care?"

"Cause the shock will knock you out, and you won't be able to work."

"Ah, I see. And who is our Warden?"

Deemus coughed. "You got lots of questions" He tapped the side of his head. "I got answers. Yup."

By this time, the others began to wake up.

Deemus moved from the shadows and sat down on an empty sleeping mat. He was dirty, his hair was shaggy and unkempt, yet his eyes shone with a manic energy.

Tem groaned and rolled over. "It's a crime to feel this bad, without the pleasure of feeling good first." He opened his eyes and saw Deemus.

"Who are you?"

"Deemus. Who are you?"

"Tem."

Deemus squinted at him.

"You don't look like a Tem. Any of them women your wives?" Demus asked.

Looking at Tem, Jon decided that deception wouldn't do them any good, so he answered truthfully. "No, but don't get any ideas."

Deemus chuckled. "Oh, all I gots is ideas. You take 'em away, ain't poor Deemus got nothing left."

Both Jona and Kiala were now awake, and had moved to the far side of the cell.

"Oh, I ain't gonna bite. My fleas might though." Deemus grinned.

When Jona made a face, Deemus frowned at her and said, "I'm just kiddin, there ain't no fleas in here." Offended, he stalked back to his corner, muttering to himself, curled up and went to sleep.

No one spoke for the next few minutes and the only sound in the cell was the sound of Deemus snoring.

Kiala whispered, "Do you think he's dangerous or insane?"

Jon said softly, "Who says he's not both? But right now, he's the only source of information we have about this place. Oh, by the way, don't touch the grid – it may be electrified."

————————

The new woman had awakened several minutes earlier, but had not spoken. She still seemed to be overwhelmed by what was happening.

Jon smiled at her and said, "My name is Jon, welcome to our little group."

The woman didn't return the smile. "My name is Anie Wallin, and I don't understand why I'm here. I was cleaning the basement for the house I clean, and my employer was angry about something. She gets angry sometimes, and then I just do the best job I can and get away from her. There were some video crystals in the basement that she had left out, and I was putting them back in a drawer, and she had left the viewer on, and I just wanted to see what was on the crystals, and it looked like that big room, and she caught me, and she was so mad..." Anie started crying again.

Kiala sat down beside her and put her arm around her. "It's OK," she said soothingly.

Jon asked, "Who do you work for?"

Tearfully, and with some pride in her voice, Anie answered, "Ms. Mercantus. She's an important government official."

Jon said, "Now we know why you're here."

Tem smiled and said to Anie, "We're all in this together."

Jona said, "If we can figure out what 'this' is."

Ignorning her, Tem said, "I wonder what time it is? I'm actually getting a little hungry."

Deemus had awoken from his nap, and was watching them warily.

"Ain't time to eat. We gets two meals a day – FirstMeal and LastMmeal. Food's not bad – once you get used to the insects crawling around in your mush."

He looked at the women and said, "Maybe I'm kidding."

Despite herself, Kiala laughed. Deemus flashed her a toothless grin.

Tem asked, "Deemus, how long have you been here?"

Deemus looked sideways at him, "You mean in this cell, or in this prison?"

"In this prison."

Deemus propped his hand up against his chin, like a philosopher preparing for a debate. "About five years, I'd say. I was one of the first to come here," he said proudly.

Jona asked him, "Why were you sent here?"

Deemus's eyes narrowed, and he spat out one word, "Mercantus."

He was silent for a long moment, then said, "Oh, I'd like to show that lump a thing or two – I'd give her the tour!"

Jona said, "She's been promoted to Group Leader of the Civil Stability Group."

Deemus's eyes grew wide with disbelief, then he let out a huge belly laugh, followed by a coughing spell.

"Well, that old sow, she knows how to get what she wants." He winked at Anie, who looked away.

Tem said, "When do we get something to eat."

Deemus looked at him and said, "Tomorrow morning. You all came in after Lastmeal."

They heard a sound like the muffled tolling of a bell. Once, twice, three times.

Deemus sniffed. "Lights out in three minutes. None of you come over here tonight. I said I didn't bite, but that's when I'm awake. I make no promises about what I do when I'm asleep."

And with that, he lay down on his mat and went straight to sleep.

Tem asked, "What do you think, should one of us watch him?"

Jon said, "I think we'll be OK. If anybody feels threatened during the night, just yell."

Jona said, "If he gets near me, you'll hear *him* yell. In pain."

Jon nodded. "I think we'll be OK."

———————

After a very unrestful night, the prisoners were awakened by another muffled bell sound – four quick rings, followed by two long slow ones.

Jon looked over at Deemus's mat – it was empty, then he looked over at the curtained area, and saw the top of Deemus's head swaying. He was singing.

After a few minutes, he opened the curtain, and stepped out, water dripping from his beard. Jon was afraid he would shake like a dog and spatter them all, but he just hummed to himself and went back to his mat.

Kiala said, "Good morning, Deemus."

Deemus looked at her as if he had never seen her before, then gave her a big smile and said, "Good morning to you too, lady!"

"Deemus, what's going to happen today?"

Steepling his hands, as if he were preparing to give a lecture, Deemus said, "First we go to FirstMeal, then we work until FirstBreak, then we work until SecondBreak, then we work until ThirdBreak, then we work until LastMeal, then we come back here for the night. Or not."

He looked confused. "Sometimes it changes."

Tem said, "I don't know about anybody else, but I could use some food right about now."

Deemus laughed and said, "You'd better hope you don't say the same thing after you eat."

Tem looked doubtfully at him. "How do we get food?"

Deemus said, "We go to the Refectory, then we eat. If you don't go to the Refectory, you don't eat, but you'd better eat, cause if you don't eat you get sick and you don't want to go to the Infirmary."

Jona asked, "Why not."

Deemus squinted at her. "I see people go in. I don't see people come out." He tapped the side of his head knowingly. "Deemus pays attention."

Kiala asked, "Where is the Infirmary?"

In the distance, they heard three short muffled sounds, followed by three muffled long sounds, then the grid enclosing their cell vanished.

As he shuffled out the door, he said, "The Infirmary's right beside the Refectory. Probably same people work in both places." He grinned. "Come on, let's go eat."

They reluctantly followed Deemus out of the cell.

The group joined a slow-moving herd of other prisoners trudging down flight after flight of transparent stairs, all heading for a low opening at the end of the cellblock.

As he looked around, Jon noticed that everyone around him had a slightly faraway expression, as if they were preoccupied with something.

Jon whispered to Tem, "Notice the demeanor of our fellow guests?"

Tem nodded. "I'd say they look like they've had an overdose of that pacification gas. Something's probably in the food they're going to give us."

"Or the water."

"Or both."

Tem whispered, "We can't go without food and water."

Jon looked back behind them. "It won't hurt you to miss a meal or two."

Kiala whispered, "Shhhh. Let's take this one meal at a time. After all, Deemus doesn't appear to be drugged."

Jon said, "That's true, but he seems to have the additional advantage of being insane."

Several yards ahead of them, Deemus looked back and said in a loud voice, "What are you perps talking about?"

Tem called out, "We were saying how much we're looking forward to breakfast."

Deemus scowled back at them but said nothing further.

Jona said, "I don't know about the rest of you, but even though I haven't eaten in awhile, I don't really have an appetite."

Deemus's description of the Infirmary, combined with the smell of the other inmates pressed so close to them, didn't help any of their appetites.

They passed through the opening in the cellblock and into a long low corridor hollowed out of rock. There were lights spaced too far apart, and the effect of so many people crammed in such a small space was almost overpoweringly claustrophobic. Jon thought, *Maybe it's a good idea so many seem sedated. With this number of people, at least a few would probably be having an anxiety attack right now.*

After several hundred yards, the tunnel began to widen, and they now found themselves in another vast open space. People ahead of them were moving toward what seemed like a large conveyor belt which had evenly spaced transparent partitions. Where the conveyor belt began was a robot guard who seemed to be making sure that only a certain number of people got into a partition.

Jon turned around and whispered quickly, "Let's stay together." They tried to push toward the front to get in the same partition as Deemus, but the press of people was just too thick. As he was herded into a partition ahead of them Deemus smiled his toothless smile and waved at them. "See you on the other side," he yelled, and moved down the belt with his group.

One more group of people was partitioned off, before Jon and his group were at the opening to the belt. Tem, Jona, and Anie stood in front, hesitating before the moving belt. In the blink of an eye, the robot extended blunt metal arms and firmly swept them into the partition. Jon and Kiala quickly followed, keeping well away from the robot. Several more people shuffled in behind them, then the robot extended its arm, and their partition began moving down the line.

The entire episode had taken less than a minute, and despite himself, Jon admired the efficiency.

"You know, if we weren't where we are, I'd say this was sort of fun," Jona said. Jon was glad that Jona seemed in a better mood. They would all be better served to stay alert and upbeat. Things would almost certainly get harder from here on in.

Jon examined the other people who had been assigned to their partition – two men and a woman. Jon spoke to the nearest man.

"Hi, my name's Jon. I'm new here."

The man looked mildly surprised that Jon was talking to him and didn't answer.

Jon decided to keep trying.

"How long have you been here?"

The man looked away, and for a moment Jon thought he was ignoring Jon's question, but then he said in a gravelly and unused voice, "Don't know."

They rode on in silence.

They entered yet another short tunnel, then came to what must have been the Refectory. They could see tables and benches to the right of the conveyor belt. Up ahead people were being swept out of their partitions and deposited in front of tables. After a few minutes, the floor of the conveyor belt began to sharply tilt toward the right, and the partition wall levered over, and swept them off the belt into another transparent partition where a long table and bench sat. The group took its cues from the other prisoners in their partition and sat down at the table.

Almost immediately, trays filled with a steaming meatloaf-looking food and cups of water appeared from panels in the table. The two men and woman immediately began eating, not hungrily, Jon observed, but also not as if they were forcing themselves to eat.

Tem leaned over and smelled the meatloaf, frowned slightly, then took a fork and gingerly tasted a bite.

The others looked at him. "Well?" Kiala finally said.

Tem tentatively tasted the water and said, "It's not bad."

Jon said, "If we can help it, let's not eat all we're given. We need to stay as sharp as we can for now."

Jona pushed her plate away. "Not a problem for me. I couldn't eat if you forced me."

Without looking at Jona, the woman beside her reached over and grabbed Jona's plate, and shared it with the two men. Jona started to protest, but Jon touched her arm, and said, "Let it go. We don't want to get on the wrong side of people our first day."

Jona grunted and sipped her water.

No one spoke or made eye contact.

After another ten minutes, the two men and woman had finished all their food, and Jon, Tem, and Kiala had eaten about a quarter of their food.

Suddenly, the bench they were all sitting on moved backwards, and the two men and woman stood up. Jon, Tem, Kiala, and Jona were still sitting when the bench and table disappeared into the floor, leaving them sprawling.

Getting up hurriedly, Jon said, "I guess lunchtime's over."

The two men and woman walked to the opposite side of the partition, which opened to reveal another conveyor belt. The wall behind Jon began to push them forward toward the belt, and they all yielded to the inevitable and stepped on the conveyor.

Instead of taking them back to their cellblock, this conveyor took them to yet another large room, this one with a much lower ceiling. People were being dumped off of the conveyor belt and began shuffling toward several carts filled with gravel. Attached to the front of the carts were what seemed to be harnesses. Several men and women in front of Jon and Tem picked up part of a harness and strapped themselves in.

"You've got to be kidding me," said Jona. "I'm not going to be a beast of burden."

Noticing the watchful robots near all the carts, Kiala said, "Let's find some good strong backs to harness up with, and get this over with."

The harnesses held quite a number of people, and so the load was really not that heavy. The robots guided the carts onto paths leading downward.

During the morning, the group pulled a loaded cart down to a dumping area, then another work group unloaded the cart, and the harness group pulled the empty cart back uphill, where yet another group filled it up again.

The pulling really wasn't that arduous. In fact, Jon found the physical labor strangely calming. He mentioned this to Tem.

"You know, this really isn't that bad. I don't know what I was expecting, but this really isn't that horrible."

Jona replied, "Just think of doing this every day for the rest of your life."

When Jon didn't respond, Jona asked him, "How do you feel? Is it possible that your...euphoria....is caused by the meatloaf you all ate?"

Jon considered this. He tried to gauge his alertness.

"I do feel a little...disconnected."

In truth, the work wasn't that hard – they had frequent breaks, and the robot guards didn't seem to mind if they walked very slowly. Even though he still felt great, Jon was a little more subdued thinking about Jona's comment.

They worked at a leisurely pace that entire afternoon, and before they knew it, several more muted bell-sounds had sounded, and they filed back onto the conveyor belt for Lastmeal.

This meal was a large bowl of some kind of watery soup and a hunk of dark bread. After drinking all of his water, Jon attacked the soup with gusto, and barely noticed that the others did the same. Everyone except Jona.

"This is the best soup I've ever had," said Jon, slurping the last drops from the bowl.

Jona frowned. "Jon, didn't you tell us not to eat everything we were given?" "Did I say that?" he asked, thinking vaguely that he did.

"Yes," Jona said. "Remember the pacification drugs?"

"Oh," he said absently. "Good soup."

When the bench slid back, they stood up like old hands, and marched right into their partition. Jon trusted the conveyor to take them back to their cellblock, and it did.

Kiala asked the group, "Do we remember the way back?"

Tem said, "I have a feeling all we have to do is look for Deemus."

Jona said, "I memorized our cell number when we left – D5 – 53427."

Jon said, "Good job." For some reason he felt as content as he had felt in a very long time. He had eaten good food, had done a good day's work, and was looking forward to a good night's sleep. Something in the back of his mind nagged at him – something was not right about this, but he couldn't put his finger on exactly what.

Deemus was waiting back for them when they got back to the cell. As the last of the group walked into the cell, the grid energized over the door.

"Had a good day, did you?" Deemus cackled.

Tem said, "It wasn't as bad as I'd thought it would be. By the way, where did you go after FirstMeal? I didn't see you in any of the workgroups."

Deemus puffed up and said, "I gots a special job." He laughed.

"You're a goldbricker," said Jona.

Delighted, Deemus clapped his hands, "You pegged me, missy. Senior Goldbricker Deemus First Class, at your service." He bowed deeply, coughed, and went to his mat.

Jon found the mat he had slept on the previous night. Was it his imagination, or did the mat feel softer? No matter. After visiting the privacy area, he came back and lay down. It did feel softer. He started to ask Kiala or Tem if they thought their mats were softer, but before he knew it, he fell fast asleep.

Chapter 6

Jon awoke in a cold sweat. He looked around, disoriented and dizzy. He swallowed and tasted hot needles. His head pounded so intensely, he felt he might be sick. He got up and stumbled to the privacy area and threw up. Sweating, he stumbled back to his mat. Was this his mat? It felt so hard, and he remembered how the mat felt before he went to sleep. Were the drugs they were giving him that potent? Apparently, he was having an allergic reaction. That could be a problem. A big problem.

He fell back into a fitful sleep.

He dreamed he was back at the water purification plant, and he and Syd were standing on the top of the first waterfall. Syd was in a buoyant mood, and playfully shouted to Jon, "Watch me," and he dove off the waterfall, doing flips on the way down. Amazed, Jon watched him tumble gracefully into the water. A few seconds later, he popped up to the surface, grinning like an idiot, and called out, "OK, now your turn."

Jon looked down at him, took off his coat, and began performing an elaborate stretching ritual.

Still treading water, Syd called out, "Quit stalling, come on down!"

Jon got a running start, and leapt off the top of the waterfall into space. But instead of falling down toward Syd he floated upwards toward the domed ceiling. Jon shut his eyes and embraced the sense of weightlessness. He opened his eyes again to see a column in the distance, growing closer and closer. He could make out bolts of light coming from the column. He was now falling toward the column, moving faster and faster. A bolt of light shot past him, missing him by inches, and he frantically tried to stop, to change direction, but he kept falling and falling...

———————

"Jon, wake up."

Jon started awake with a sickening sense of vertigo. It took him several seconds to realize he was back in the cell. It was morning.

"It's OK, it's just us," said Tem. "You look pale, do you feel OK?"

"A little sick. How do you all feel?"

Tem considered the question, then answered, "Fit and ready for work. After FirstMeal, of course."

"Tem, we have to keep trying to find a way out of here," Jon said.

The younger man looked at him strangely, then said, "Yes, of course."

Jon looked over at Kiala, who had just returned from the privacy corner, "Kiala, how do you feel?"

She frowned. "I don't feel bad at all, and I know I should. I had a good sleep, and now I'm hungry."

Worried now, Jon began to ask Jona the same thing, but before he could speak, she said, "I feel terrible, weak, and hungry, and you would have to hold me down to make me eat any of that food. Don't you all see what's happening?"

Jon said, "Yes," but the other two just looked confused. Jon looked over at Anie, who was still asleep. She looked pale, and her breathing was shallow. Jon suspected that she might be allergic to the pacification drug as well.

Jona sat down beside Jon. "It seems that we have a mystery."

"What?"

She gestured toward the corner that Deemus had appropriated. He was curled up in a ball and snoring. "He doesn't appear to be affected by the drug – why is that?"

Jon scratched his head, "Don't know. Let's ask him when he wakes up."

Kiala and Tem waited by the opening of the cell. They were obviously eager to get back down for some FirstMeal meatloaf.

Looking at them with concern, Jona said, "OK, the good news is we can assume that the water they're giving us contains none of the drug."

"Maybe the water contains small amounts that will build up in our systems over time," Jon said.

Jona frowned. "And you think I'm a pessimist?"

"We have to find a way out of here," she added.

Still feeling sick, Jon agreed. "I think that some people have a toxic reaction to the drug."

Jona looked at him, "You threw up last night."

"Yeah. I feel a little better today, but I'm definitely weaker. In a few days at most, I'll have to eat, or risk being taken to the Infirmary."

Jona shrugged. "Rumor has it that's not a good alternative."

Jon looked over at the still sleeping Anie. "She looks like she also had a bad reaction to the food."

Jona said, "Yeah. I don't think I can hold out much longer without food myself."

"So how do we get out of here."

"You want to leave this beautiful place?" said Deemus lightly.

Both Jon and Jona jumped. "How long have you been listening to us?" Jona demanded.

Deemus laughed and said, "When did I stop snoring? I know I snore," he added defensively.

Jona said, "You don't have that glassy-eyed look that the other prisoners here have. Why not?"

Deemus rubbed his hands together. "Oh, Deemus don't like meatloaf. Nope."

Jona gritted her teeth. "You have to eat something; what do you eat?"

Deemus smiled. "Deemus works in the kitchen, he gets almost-warden food," he said proudly.

"You mean food that the prison staff eats?"

"Yup, not meatloaf."

Jon said, "I haven't seen any human prison staff here, just the automatons."

Deemus shrugged, "Don't come in here much; they work other places."

"I'm going to get some scrambled eggs," Deemus said. "With cheese."

Both Jona and Jon felt their stomachs rumbling.

Jon asked, "Deemus, do you think you could get us some of that food?"

Deemus said, "Why, don't you like meatloaf?" He laughed.

"We don't want to turn into zombies," said Jona before Jon could shush her.

Quickly Jon added, "The meatloaf make some of us sick."

Deemus nodded wisely, "Yup, I've seen that happen to people. Then they go to Infirmary, never come back," he added sadly.

"But you could get us some food that wouldn't make us sick, right?" asked Jona hopefully. "You don't want us to go to the Infirmary, do you?"

"Maybe," said Deemus.

"You don't want us to go to the Infirmary, do you?" Jona pressed.

"No," said Deemus, a little peevishly

Jon said, "OK, can we go get that food now?"

Deemus thought for a moment, then said, "OK, when the bell for FirstMeal sounds, follow me."

Jona said, "What about Kiala and Tem?" They were still obediently waiting beside the door.

Deemus said, "It looks like they like meatloaf."

Jon said to Jona, "We need to take Anie with us too."

Jona said, "I'll wake her. Hold on."

Jona knelt by the sleeping woman and shook her gently awake.

"How do you feel?" Jona asked.

"Like I need to throw up again."

Deemus wrinkled his nose. "Then hurry up, we need to go soon."

Anie made a face. "Go where? Back to the Refectory? I think it was the food that made me sick!"

Jona said, "We're going to try to find some food that won't make us sick, but we need to hurry."

Anie got up unsteadily and headed for the privacy corner.

The Firstmeal bell sounded, and Tem and Kiala were out the door as soon as the grid deactivated. Deemus said, "OK, follow me."

Jona called out, "Anie, come on, we need to leave."

They ran to catch up to Deemus.

The group joined the jostling throng as they shuffled through the same access doorway they had gone through the day before. Every so often, Deemus would look back at them. Jon began to wonder if this was a bad idea. His empty stomach ended the argument.

By this time, Tem and Kiala were far ahead of them in another partition.

Jona grabbed Jon's sleeve. "What about Tem and Kiala?"

Jon said, "We'll have to catch up to them in the work area."

Like the day before, they were swept into a partition on the conveyor. But somehow, Deemus managed to secure a partition containing just their small group – one less than yesterday.

As they were traveling toward the Refectory, Deemus lowered his voice conspiratorially. "OK, you pay attention. When the wall comes to sweep you to your table, just pick your feet up, lean back, and turn to your left. You'll roll right over the wall. It's easier than it sounds. Just watch me, and do what I do. I'll tell you when."

They entered the Refectory and Jon saw the tables at the far end filling up. Their turn would be very soon.

As Jon felt the wall gently begin to push him toward the tables, Deemus said, "Now, pick you feet up, lean and roll!" Jon and Jona did as he instructed and amazingly found themselves on the opposite side of the wall.

Anie had not been quick enough, and was being swept out of the partition. Jon reached over, grabbed her by her shoulders, and pulled her over the wall. She squealed with fright.

"It's OK, we're all OK." They found themselves in an upward-sloping corridor that ran the length of the conveyor belt. Deemus waited impatiently ahead of them. Mimicking Jon's voice, he said, "'OK, we're all OK'. Come on then."

He led them down the corridor and stopped in front of a door with a keypad lock. He deftly entered a series of numbers, and the door opened. Jon glanced over at Jona, who had quietly positioned herself so she had a clear view of the keypad. She winked at him.

They followed Deemus through the doorway into another corridor with windows opening onto the Refectory. They were now several feet above the floor level in the Refectory.

"Stay here," said Deemus, and disappeared through another locked door ahead on the left.

John asked Jona, "Did you get the keycodes?"

She grinned and said, "Hey, that's my job."

With Deemus gone, they had a chance to stop and look down at the Refectory. Jon said, I don't remember seeing any windows on this wall from the outside, I mean, inside."

"One-way glass?" Jona guessed.

"If we get caught, we're in big trouble." said Anie.

They all looked at each other.

Jona said, "Aw, come on. Don't tell me you've never sneaked food from the kitchen before?"

Anie laughed. "Ok, you got me. I confess – I stole peanut butter from Medusa Mercantus."

At the mention of their tormentor's name, the group fell silent.

"Well," Jon said, "let's see if we can work on arranging a reunion with our patron so we can thank her for allowing us to stay here."

"That would be nice," said Jona.

"I never want to see her again," said Anie.

Deemus poked his head out the door and said, "The coast is clear, come on then."

They followed him into a room that very much resembled a normal kitchen – refrigeration unit, fast and slow cooking units, washing units.

Deemus rummaged through a storage locker. "How about some pancakes with syrup?"

Anie said, "That sounds good."

He handed her the tray, and she went over to one of the fast cooking units, and popped the tray into the slot.

She turned to Deemus and said, "Now you're sure that this food doesn't have that, that..."

"Pacification drug," said Jon

"Pacification drug," repeated Anie.

Deemus shook his head, "Nope, I eat 'em all the time, and I'm as alert as a warden." He stood up a little straighter and puffed out his chest.

Jona began searching though the locker that Deemus had just opened.

Sounding a little miffed that she was taking charge, Deemus said, "Help yourself."

Jona said, "Sorry, it's just that I haven't eaten anything in several days."

Deemus nodded and said, "Oh. That explains why you're always grumpy, then."

Jon laughed, and Jona muttered, "Right."

Jon said, "OK, so what have we got?"

Jona read the labels on the trays she had pulled out: "Ham, eggs, cheese, and potatoes...."

Jon reached for the tray. "Sold." He headed toward a free cooking unit.

Jona said, "There are meals in here to last us quite a while."

Happily devouring her pancakes, Anie asked, "Is there any coffee?"

Deemus mumbled something, and said in a louder voice, "I'll go look."

Jona said, "I don't know if he's quite comfortable with the waiter gig yet."

Tearing off the top of his tray to reveal a steaming piece of ham and soft scrambled eggs, Jon said, "I think he's doing a fine job."

A few minutes later, Deemus came back with self-heating cups of coffee and some juice bulbs.

It seemed like a feast.

Jon realized that they had been so focused on getting something to eat and drink that they really might be in some danger. For some reason, he had trusted Deemus, and so far, Deemus had come through admirably.

"Deemus," he said, "we appreciate your help."

Deemus stopped eating his pancakes and looked up warily.

"You heard us talking this morning about escaping? Do you know if there's a way to escape from here? Maybe other people have tried?"

Deemus put his fork down and looked up at the ceiling. "Not up. Up is too hard, too many guards. Mean guards," he winced.

Jona asked, "What about going horizontally, to the edge of the prison, then up?"

Deemus shook his head, "Nope, prison's too big – maybe hundreds of cellblocks just like ours. Too big." He licked his fork. "I like pancakes."

Jon and Jona were stunned. "Hundreds of cellblocks like this one. That's hundreds of thousands of people."

Deemus scratched his beard, "I guess old Medusa didn't get along with a lot of people."

Deemus looked thoughtful.

"There is one other direction."

"What?" said Jon.

"Down."

"Down?"

Deemus opened a second coffee cup. "Yep, Down is Out."

He frowned as he looked into the cup.

"I need sugar and cream," he said, and left to go find some.

Jona said, "Just when you think he's talking like he knows what he's talking about, he goes wobbly."

Jon shrugged. "He's all we've got."

After a few minutes, Deemus returned with some cream and sugar. He reheated his coffee, added generous amounts of both substances, and sipped the concoction.

"Yup, Down. But watch yourselves. Down is dangerous, with the Labyrinth down there, but it seems to me that if a person really, really wanted to leave, then Down is Out."

Jon asked, "What's the Labyrinth?"

Deemus said, "Sometimes, if you're not sick, you're just trouble, the Wardens will send you to the Labyrinth. People never come back from the Labyrinth either."

He took another sip of coffee and sat back. "The prison wasn't the first thing to be built here. I heard that the prison was built on top of something else – a whole underground city. Experimental something-or-other. Geo-something."

"Geothermal?" prompted Jon.

Deemus said, "Could be. Anyhow, whole thing's secret. Lots of people, lots of money."

"So what happened?" asked Jona.

Deemus coughed, spilling some of his coffee on the table.

"Pffft, how would I know?" he said. "Do I look like a Project Manager?" He grinned wickedly, coffee dribbling down his chin.

"You never told us what you did to get sent here."

Deemus looked down at the floor. "No, I didn't."

"Well?" asked Anie.

"Well what?" countered Deemus.

"Why did you get sent here?"

Deemus stood up. "Shhh, I hear footsteps."

Nobody moved.

For the first time since they had met Deemus, the old man seemed genuinely afraid and uncertain.

The footsteps seemed to be coming from the corridor, in the opposite direction from which they had come.

Deemus said, "Quick, Put your trays and cups in the recycler, and don't make no noise."

As quietly as possible, they cleaned up. Demus crept toward the door, listened for a second, then said, "Follow me."

He led them back through the kitchen area through a door that lead to a warehouse/storage area filled with boxes and cylinders.

Looking back toward the kitchen, Deemus said, "Hurry, get behind those boxes at the back of the room."

Obediently, they followed his instructions. As they crouched behind the boxes, Jona pointed to some nearby cylinders. "Look at the labels," she whispered.

"Civil Stabilty-approved pacification drugs. Enough for thousands of people."

"Shhh," whispered Deemus. "This place echoes, you wanna get caught?"

They kept silent.

After several uncertain minutes, Deemus got up and whispered, "I'll see if they're gone. You stay here and don't say nothing."

He scuttled off, and Jon, Anie, and Jona looked at each other.

Deemus came back and said, "OK, nobody's around now. I'll show you the passage to go to the work area."

Jona pointed to an opening in the far wall. "Where does that go?"

Deemus looked distinctly uncomfortable.

"Deemus, tell us, where does that passage lead?"

Deemus held his head in his hands, as if he had just gotten a terrible headache. "OK, you want to know?"

"Yes we do," said Jona gently.

"It goes to the Labyrinth."

They all looked at him.

Anie asked, "Have you ever gone down there?"

He looked at her with a mixture of pity and disgust. "I'm crazy – I ain't stupid."

He led them back through the kitchen to the corridor. "Go to the end and through the door. You'll be in the passageway that leads to a cart loading area. Just go through. Then go to work."

Jon asked, "But won't that look strange, us showing up in the middle of the morning?"

Deemus looked at him. "No, nobody cares, as long as people leave the cellblocks in the morning.

Wardens don't much check up on folks digging out new tunnels. Robots keep people working."

Jona looked down the corridor. "Is it safe? I mean could we get caught by whoever was here before?"

Deemus shrugged. "Don't think so, there ain't no connecting corridors down that way, and the staff don't go near the tunnels – they let the robots handle the tunnel guarding."

Anie asked, "Where will you go?"

Deemus grinned crookedly. "You got your job, I got my job. Seeya."

And without another word, he scuttled off in the opposite direction.

Jon looked at Jona and Anie. "Well, I guess we'd better not wait around. We've trusted Deemus this far, there's no reason to stop now."

Jona said, "Yeah, let's get going."

They set off at a brisk walk toward the tunnels.

The door leading out was exactly where Deemus said it was, unlocked from this side. Jon pushed the door open and they found themselves in a small side tunnel that lead to the loading area they had been in the day before. After Jona and Anie stepped though the door, it swiftly closed. From this side, it was impossible to tell that the door existed.

They quickly moved to the loading area. As Deemus predicted, no one commented on their arrival; in fact no one even noticed their presence. They walked up to a loaded cart that had several harness positions empty, harnessed up, and when the automaton indicated they should start pulling, they made their way up the tunnel.

As they walked up the tunnel, Jona said, "I wonder where Tem and Kiala are."

Jon looked around, "I don't know, we'll probably have to wait until tonight to see them."

Anie said, "By then, they'll have had two more meals – more drugs."

Frustrated, Jon said, "There's nothing we can do about that."

Jona said, "Yes there is, we can take them with us when we go tomorrow."

Jon considered this. "I don't know. What if they don't want to come. At this point, we don't know enough about how the drug works, how quickly it leaves the system. Let's just wait until tonight and see how they are."

The rest of the day passed much as the day before. The work was more boring than difficult. They were allowed plenty of rest. During one of these rest breaks, Jon walked over and tried to make conversation with the man who had been in harness beside him. Although they had worked together for most of the day, the man didn't seem to recognize Jon when he spoke to him.

Jon said, "This work is pretty easy, isn't it."

The man looked at him in mild surprise, then looked down at his feet and grunted.

Jon tried again. "Have you been here long? Have you done other work here besides this?"

This time, the man didn't even acknowledge Jon, he just got up and shuffled back to his harness.

Jona and Anie came up to Jon. "Any luck talking to the natives?"

"None whatsoever."

At the end of the work shift, they lingered with the empty carts as the rest of the inmates shuffled toward the Refectory. Deemus had told them that the automatons would not force them to go to the Refectory for Lastmeal – they could wait at the work area until Lastmeal was over, then they could follow the rest of the prisoners back to their cell block.

Jona said, "I'm getting a little hungry."

"Me too," Anie agreed.

Jon watched the last of the inmates leave. "It would be better if we could wait until tomorrow and let Deemus guide us again. I don't want to take any unnecessary chances."

"We can go back by ourselves. I have all the access codes," Jona said.

"Let's keep that plan in reserve. Deemus still knows more about how security works down here than we do. We might be able to find the kitchen again, but if somebody caught us...." He let the thought trail away. "I think we'd be safer sticking with Deemus for now."

Jona sighed. "OK, fine." She looked down. "Hear that stomach?"

They waited for the bell to announce the end of Lastmeal, and the return to the cellblock. Finally, the bell sounded, and soon hundreds of workers began shuffling past them toward the cell blocks. It was no problem to blend in with the crowd.

Presently, they returned to their cellblock, and climbed back toward their cell. "Home sweet home," said Jona as she slumped down on her mat.

Anie looked around. "Where's Deemus?" she asked.

"That's odd," said Jona. "He was here last night when we got here."

Just then, Tem and Kiala shuffled in. They looked mildly surprised to see Jon, Jona, and Anie, but said nothing. Kiala headed toward the privacy corner, and Tem sat down on his mat.

Jon came over and sat down beside Tem.

"Hi Tem, how are you?"

For a few seconds, Tem didn't say anything. Then he briefly looked up and said, "OK."

Jon continued, "Did you have a good day?"

With an effort, Tem said, "Yes."

Jon felt as if he was talking to an extremely slow and sleepy child. "Tem, didn't you worry about us when we didn't come to the Refectory with you?"

Briefly, Tem looked puzzled, then smiled. "Good food. I like the food."

Jon said, "OK, You're probably tired, so I'll let you sleep."

"Tired," agreed Tem and lay down on his mat. He fell asleep almost instantly.

Jona had been trying to talk to Kiala across the cell, with apparently the same success.

After Kiala fell asleep, Jona, Jon, and Anie sat down on their mats.

"They're pretty much out of it," said Anie.

Jona agreed. "I just had no idea it would work so fast."

Wearily, Jon said, "I guess it was a matter of expediency for the Wardens. If you could control the prisoners for twenty-four hours, you'd be guaranteed to have a docile, obedient workforce from then on."

Just then, the security grid activated, casting a faint, deadly light.

Jona said, "It seems somebody didn't come home tonight."

Deemus's corner was empty.

Anie said, "Do you think something happened to him?"

Jon frowned. "Probably not. Deemus, for all his instability, seems to be a survivor. He's probably in a nice, warm nest somewhere, surrounded by empty food trays."

Jona groaned. "Thanks for the mental picture."

Anie persisted, "But what if he doesn't come back?"

Jona scowled at her and said, "That would be a mixed blessing, I'd say."

Jon lay back on his cot and looked at the ceiling. "Well, we did learn a lot today – the way around the Refectory, the kitchen..." He paused.

"You're not thinking what I think you're thinking," Jona began.

"What?" asked Anie."

Jona looked at Jon. "The passageway to the Labyrinth."

Jon propped himself up on one elbow. "You heard him yourself: Down is Out."

Jona stared at him. "Are you crazy? Did you also hear him say that the Wardens banish people down there? They never come back."

"Maybe they found ways to escape?"

Jona snorted. "Not bloody likely. Plus, what can we take down there for protection, light, food, water, maybe even air?"

Jon lay back and closed his eyes.

"Okay, okay. It's a moot point for now anyway. We need to figure out how to carry our two model workers with us."

The lights in the cellblock grew dimmer and dimmer.

"Let's all get some sleep. Tomorrow's another day."

———————

Jon awoke with a start the next morning. The others were already up, and Tem and Kiala stood beside the door waiting for breakfast.

Jona asked Jon, "Sleep well?"

"Better than the night before. How about you, Anie?"

"I'm not sick anymore, just hungry."

"That's good."

The bell announcing Firstmeal sounded, and the grid deactivated, but before Tem and Kiala could shuffle out, Deemus ran into the cell.

"Deemus, where were you last night?"

The old man hurried toward the privacy corner, and said, "Fell asleep at the job. By the time I woke up, lights were out, and Security was turned on. Listen, if you get caught outside the cellblock after lights out, don't come back in. The cameras will see you and you...well just don't do it."

"I also heard that our Warden is coming to the Refectory today, so we can't go to the kitchen – security will be extra tight, and you don't want to get caught, do you?"

Anie said, "But what about the meatloaf? It makes me and Jon sick."

Like a snappish schoolteacher, Deemus looked at her and said, "Just give it to someone else."

"But what will we eat?"

Deemus looked at her and said, "You're not skin and bones. You'll survive another day."

Tem and Kiala had already left just after Deemus came in, and the others followed behind.

As they approached the conveyor, Deemus whispered, "We'd better split up, there'll be more people to give your food to without getting caught."

Jon ended up in a partition with Kiala. She looked right through him.

Jon said, "Kiala, do you remember me?"

She looked at him, blinked several times, and finally said, "Jon."

"Yes, that's right. And you remember your own name, right?"

She blinked in concentration several more times, then finally said, "No."

A cold shudder ran down Jon's spine. "You're Kiala."

She looked at him and said, "Yes, Kiala." Then she turned away.

Tem, Deemus, and Jona were in the partition ahead of them.

When they were deposited at their tables, Jon could just see them through the milky Plexiglas.

Deemus waved at him, then looked stricken and sat down quickly. Confused, Jon looked over his shoulder at a bubble descending from the ceiling.

Inside the bubble were several heavily armed human guards and one finely-dressed man. Jon guessed that he was their Warden.

The bubble slowly hovered over each of the tables, passing over Jon's table in turn. Kiala was busily eating the food on her tray, and he picked up a forkful and pretended to eat it. The bubble moved on to Deemus's table. Jon stopped pretending to chew and watched as the bubble moved closer to Deemus's table. Jona had also been pretending to eat her food, and was making a show of moving food around on her plate.

To Jon's surprise, the bubble descended to the Refectory floor and the Warden got out and walked over to Jona.

Watching him approach out of the corner of her eye, Jona picked up a forkful of food and ate it, very slowly.

The Warden smiled at her, and made a hand gesture to his guards. The guards immediately seized Jona. Too surprised to cry out, she struggled with them as they carried her back to the bubble. When they were all inside, the bubble swiftly ascended to an opening in the ceiling.

A bell rang and they were swept back on the conveyor.

———————

When the conveyor deposited them at the work site, Jon ran over to Deemus and grabbed him by his shoulders. "What happened? Who was that? Where did he take Jona? Tell me!"

Deemus squirmed out of Jon's grip.

"No problems, the Warden ain't gonna hurt her. Probably not. Anyway," he shook his head like a dog. "It's her problem, not my problem."

Jon grabbed him again. "I'm your problem now. Talk. Was that the Warden who took her?"

"Let me go and I'll tell you." Deemus said.

Jon released him and Deemus stepped back and tried to regain his composure. "The Warden does that sometimes – comes down here and picks a special inmate to 'interview.'"

"What do you mean, 'interview.'"

Anie said darkly, "You know what he means."

Deemus said defensively, "He never really hurts anybody. I can tell you, he's a lot better than some wardens in the other cellblocks; I've heard stories..."

Jon interrupted him. "Where did he take her?"

"Probably back to his suites."

"How do we get there?"

Deemus looked shocked. "We can't go there."

Jon said in frustration, "We can't just do nothing."

Deemus grinned and said, "Sure we can; I do it all the time."

Chapter 7

Jona looked down on the Refectory as the bubble she traveled in with the Warden and his guards floated up through the ceiling. She saw Deemus and Jon and Anie staring up at her before they were swept into the conveyor.

She glanced over at her captor, Lar Dakol, who smiled back at her and patted her knee.

"My dear, I want to assure you again that we just want to make sure that you're in good health and are having no problems adjusting to life here in our facility."

"No problems," said Jona dully. Struggling with the guards had been a huge mistake – Dakol had been surprised by her resistance. She needed to behave as compliantly as any other inmate. Despite her act, her heart was racing.

The warden's bubble traveled through special access corridors above the refectory, work areas, and cellblock that made up the warden's domain.

At one point, they came out into an open area, some kind of transportation hub, where Jona could see the tops of other cellblocks, extending for miles in all directions. Involuntarily, she sucked in her breath at the sight.

Peering intently at her, Dakol asked, "Is anything wrong?"

Thinking quickly, she said in a monotone, "Don't like heights."

With a paternal smile, Dakol said, "Ah, poor thing, we'll see you are moved to a lower level in the cellblock. Now would that be good?"

She swallowed and said slowly, "OK."

Her heat sank as they traveled over the cellblocks. Each one was encased in solid rock, with heavily-guarded tunnels providing the only connections. Even from this vantage, there was no way to tell how close to the surface they were. There were simply too many unknowns.

Finally, the bubble came to a stop outside a fortified building built right into the rock. The warden stepped off the bubble first, followed by Jona with a guard firmly holding each arm. She could fake a faint, but they would just carry her. At least they hadn't restrained her arms.

A man in a lab coat met them at the entrance, and the Warden stepped forward and spoke to him. They looked back at her, and she quickly looked down at the ground. She strained to hear what the warden and the man were saying.

The man grinned and said something she couldn't make out.

The warden snapped, "Never mind that, I want to know why she seems to be immune to the pacification treatment. When the guards selected her, she fought like a wildcat. I want to know why."

"Yes sir."

"We can't have unpacified prisoners walking around, is that clear?"

"Yes, sir."

"And," the warden added, "you'll confine your examination of her to what is medically necessary. Do I make myself clear?"

The technician's face grew red, "Yes, sir."

"When you've finished your evaluation, bring her to my office."

"Yes, sir."

The warden entered the building, followed by two more guards.

The technician walked up to Jona and said in a syrupy sweet voice, "Well, hello, how are you today?"

Jona looked at the ground, and said in a small voice, "OK."

The technician stared at her for a few seconds, then said to the guards, "Bring her this way."

This must be the main Administration building, Jona thought. *There must be weapons here, schematics, blueprints, computers that can be hacked, access codes that can be stolen...*

The technician and guards took her through winding corridors, and she concentrated on memorizing what she could of the layout of the building.

The technician stopped in front of a small room. "Put her in there."

As they shoved her into the room, the technician smiled and said, "Don't worry, I'll be back in a few minutes," and closed and locked the door.

She looked around, trying not to look too curious, in case cameras were watching her. An examination table, two chairs, a table with a small medscanner, antiseptic field generators. Not much.

She decided to sit on the examination table to wait for the technician.

After a few minutes, the technician returned with one of the guards and a fairly large medkit.

"Sorry to keep you waiting." He waved the antiseptic wand over her arm, and took out a blood evaluation kit.

"Now, to begin with, we're just going to take a sample of your blood."

He wrapped the device around her arm. She felt a brief prick as a probe inserted itself into a vein. After a few moments, a summary of her major blood chemistry appeared on a tablet the technician held.

The technician studied the display for a few moments, then shook his head a muttered to himself.

"This can't be right. There's only a trace amount of the drug in her system." He looked up suspiciously at Jona.

"Have you been eating?" he asked sharply.

She nodded. "Meatloaf good." Ugh.

Frowning, he took some more notes.

He pressed a communicator button on his collar. "Warden Dalkol?"

After a pause, the warden answered, "What is it?"

"I've completed an initial blood chemistry, and it appears that she only has trace elements of the pacification drug in her system. My theory is that her liver is somehow able to remove the toxin faster than it can be absorbed by the brain. I'd like to do more tests to confirm..."

"You idiot," the warden interrupted him. "The simplest explanation is that she just hasn't been eating."

"But the summary shows that she has eaten in the last day, and her initial arrival to the facility was two days ago..."

"Then she's found food somewhere else. Restrain her, get her pacification levels up to normal and send her up here. Do it now."

The channel went dead.

Seizing the opportunity, Jona sprang from the table, slipped underneath the guard's grasp, and kicked his feet out from under him. She opened the door and slammed it on the surprised technician, deftly scrambling the lock.

She sprinted down the corridor, frantically looking for directional signs, closets, or open doorways to duck into.

The corridor ended up ahead, leading into another that ran at right angles to this one. She had a choice to make: left or right. She chose right, and accelerated around the corner...

And ran straight into a squad of robotic sentries. Instinctively she flattened herself against the wall, and to her amazement, they hovered right past her. She paused for a second to let her heart start beating again. From what she could tell, she was probably moving farther away from the entrance, but she figured there must be another exit somewhere.

She tried a few doors but didn't try to hack the doors with number locks – that might tip off someone to her location.

Another intersection – this time she looked very carefully before deciding which way to go. Heading left this time, she saw an open door. No lights were on, so she crept in, closed the door and turned on the lights.

She was in a storage room, filled with broken computer parts, frayed optical cable, and cleaning supplies. Across the room was another door. She hurried over and put her ear against the door, listening for any sound from the other side. She opened the door just a crack, and looked out. Another corridor, parallel to the one she had just come from.

She opened the door a little wider and peered out, looking both ways.

Satisfied the coast was clear; she turned off the light, stepped out into the corridor and shut the door behind her.

She heard muffled voices coming from the other corridor she had just come from, and started running in the opposite direction.

Up ahead was a lift and a stairwell. Which one? She watched the doors of the lift open. Which way should she go? Up or down. She paused. She stepped in to the lift, pressed the indicator to the top floor and jumped out just as the door closed. They would expect her to go up, so she would go down. She ran to the stairwell. One flight down. Locked door. Two flights. Another locked door. Maybe this wasn't such a good idea after all.

Three flights. This time the door was unlocked. She peeked into the dimly-lit corridor. She heard sounds of distant machines. The air smelled damp and musty. Good, hopefully this was an unused and unmonitored area of the building. She crept steadily toward the end of the corridor, passing numbered rooms, all locked. She reached the end of the hallway and leaned over to peek around the corner when suddenly a hand reached out and grabbed her by the collar. She was lifted to her feet by a massive guard and dropped directly in front of a malevolently smiling Warden Dakol.

Chapter 8

"Excellent job, Ms. Altsul, quite excellent. I enjoyed your little performance immensely. He pointed to a small camera affixed unobtrusively on each light fixture.

Strong arms pinned Jona's arms behind her, securing her hands with restraints

"You were monitoring me the whole time," she said dully.

"In my job, it's not wise to leave anything to chance. Also, given the staff I have to work with..." Just then the technician that Jona has escaped from arrived, red-faced and puffing.

Dakol looked thoughtful. "You know, I might even have to make a regular event out of this. Take a resourceful girl and withhold our, er, 'control measures' for a time..."

"However, I'm afraid I can't imagine that most of our guests would provide the same level of entertainment you have."

"I'd bet you'd be afraid to try," Jona said.

Dakol laughed, "You don't mess with a winning strategy, little girl. Do you know what you are a part of here?" He spread his arms wide.

"Tell me," Jona said evenly.

"A solution."

"A solution," Jona repeated.

"Exactly. Our society depends upon civil harmony to function effectively. Yet, all the advantages our great system bestows on every citizen, some insist on acting in ways that hurt the collective."

"And who defines what 'hurts' the collective?"

"Our leaders, of course."

"Elected, with full knowledge and participation of an informed citizenry?"

The warden laughed again. "You are delightfully naive."

"We don't believe that the citizenry as a group has the necessary perspective, knowledge or experience."

"So the few know what's best for the many."

"Always has been, always will be."

"Not always, just in the last few years, which seem to coincide with the rising fortunes of Medusa Mercantus."

The warden's eyebrows rose.

"You are full of surprises. But don't you see what an elegant solution this is? Malcontents like you are taken out of the system, and made to do useful labor."

"Digging tunnels like rats?"

"The tunnels have to be dug, and you have to admit, we don't work people very hard."

"What about the Labyrinth?" Jona asked, and instantly regretted it.

Angrily, the warden grabbed her, and said, "Sometimes, you are just too smart for your own good."

"Well, I've enjoyed this little chat." He shoved her toward the technician and said, "Now, pacify her and bring her to me. If she gets away from you this time, I'll send you to the Labyrinth in her place. Understood?"

The technician gulped and led Jona away.

Chapter 9

Strapped down on the table in the same room she had escaped from, Jona struggled against the straps, but there was no question of getting away this time. There were now two guards beside the door. The technician was taking no chances.

"Now lie back and relax," The technician grimly measured the dosage of the drug and prepared the syringe. "You almost cost me a trip to the Labyrinth." His voice shook.

"And that scares you?" she asked.

He looked at her in amazement. "It would scare any sane person."

"What's down there that's so bad?"

"Nobody really knows, but I've heard rumors of genetic experiments gone bad, cannibals, toxic waste spills, radiation spills, unbreathable atmosphere, cave-ins, oh, it's a garden spot, you'll love it."

"Cannibals? You mean people live down there?"

"So I've heard, if your definition of 'people' is sufficiently broad."

"And nobody comes back?"

The technician smiled grimly as he stuck the needle into Jona's arm.

"Nobody."

Jona's eyes rolled back into her head. The technician checked her vital signs – administering such a large dose at once wasn't recommended, but he wasn't about to contradict the warden again. If she didn't have a heart attack in the next fifteen minutes, she'd be right as rain.

He checked her breathing, and heart rate – slightly elevated, but no signs of overdose. He stepped to a wall communicator. "Warden, she's ready."

The guards wheeled her, still strapped down, to the Warden's suite.

On the way, she became conscious again. She felt as if she was under water. She felt disconnected – not sleepy, or numb, but things were....fuzzy and hot. She knew she should fight this feeling, but somehow, she didn't know why.

The guards wheeled her table into a large and sumptuous suite, with a picture window that ran the entire length of the outer wall. From here, you could see almost the entire cellblock area.

Dakol walked over to her, picked up her hand, and released it. It dropped limply to her side.

"I think she's ready to be interviewed. You can leave us."

The guards looked at each other and left.

Dakol walked to the door and locked it.

"So we won't be disturbed."

"Now, you've proven to be an enormously resourceful girl, so it would be a waste to send you to the Labyrinth."

"One-way trip," said Jona, slurring her words.

"Exactly. My goodness, you are a quick study. Now, let's see about getting you in a more comfortable position."

He loosened the straps binding her arms and legs. She tried to move her arms, but they felt like they were disconnected from her body.

He picked her up, but she was so limp that she almost slid out of his grasp. She stumped her toe on the wheel of the table, and a stab of pain shot through her. Somehow the pain cut through her numbness and she pushed him back as hard as she could.

Dakol gasped and fell backwards, hitting his head on the side of his desk. He fell to the floor and didn't move.

Jona fell right beside him, still not able to move her legs. She lay there for an eternity, terrified that someone would find them at any moment. She fought the drug, and slowly realized that pain could temporarily clear her head.

She crawled to the still unconscious warden and searched through his pockets. Finding an access card, she bit her wrist until she winced, then tried to stand. She found that, with an effort, she could just make it to the warden's desk, where she fell into his chair exhausted. She took several deep breaths and opened his desk, searching through papers and crystals. In a bottom drawer, she got lucky. She found an old bottle of a coffee-substitute stimulant. She took half the pills in the bottle.

After several minutes she began to feel her feet. She tried to stand up, and managed to stumble back around the desk. Using some restraints she had found in his desk, she secured his hands and feet.

The coffee-substitute pills were now beginning to kick in, and she started to feel really edgy and nauseated at the same time. It wasn't a welcome feeling, but it beat limp and paralyzed.

Holding on to the desk, she stumbled back to warden's chair. Using his access card, she logged into his private system. She first downloaded a floor plan of the building to a crystal and then went trolling through his files. There it was in front of her – a program that allowed him access to any of the thousands of cameras in the facility – in this building, in the cellblock, in the Refectory, anywhere.

It was the work of a few minutes to access the underlying scripts and write a few timer programs that would replay the recordings made twenty-four hours earlier. She hacked the timestamps so the recordings would seem to be real-time, and erased her tracks.

It might have been the adrenaline rush of hacking again, or it might have been the pills she had taken, but she now felt pretty good. She could even stagger at a decent pace.

She found a data tablet and a courier bag from a closet. She filled the bag with the tablet and the crystal with the downloaded information, a few other empty crystals, the bottle of pills, and a bulb of water. There were no weapons anywhere in the suite. Still, this was better than what she had to work with an hour earlier.

She checked the empty corridor and began her escape from the Administration building. She had to find her friends.

Chapter 10

The work shift was over and Jon, Anie, Tem, and Kiala plodded toward the Refectory. Jon hadn't seen Deemus since the morning.

Anie tried to cheer Jon up.

"Maybe she'll be in the cell when we get back."

"Maybe."

"Should we try to get to the kitchen?"

"Yeah, I think that would be a good idea."

———————

Jona moved steadily through the hallways, using the camera program from her tablet to see when the coast was clear. She still felt edgy and nauseated, and at least her head was clearing. If she could get out of here, she'd be fine.

Hiding in a closet, she tried to discover whether the computer had an inmate search function. Frustrated, she said out loud, "I wish I could find Jon."

The tablet answered, "Please give last name."

Annoyed, Jona asked, "You have a voice-recognition mode?"

"Yes. Please give last name to 'Jon' to begin search or say 'Cancel' to cancel request."

"What if his last name is 'Cancel?'"

"Not understood, please restate request."

"Never mind." *What was Jon's last name? Something with a P. Patten, Plova, Preenim, Prospero, that's it – Prospero.*

"Find Jon Prospero. General population search. Go."

"Please stand by."

In a matter of seconds the search program had found Jon among what must have been tens of thousands of inmates.

The camera showed Jon with Anie, Tem, and Kiala heading toward the Refectory. They were still together; that was good.

Jona paused and queried the camera-controller program again.

"Query, can you edit out individuals from your search program?"

"Yes, there are lists of command-level personnel who are not tracked by this program."

"Good, Add additional 'command-level personnel' to the list."

"Please list names."

She did.

The computer responded, "Confirmed. Names added to list."

She giggled. Computers were so stupid.

———

Jon and Anie had managed to catch up with Tem and Kiala and were about three partitions away from entering the conveyor when Anie saw her.

She grabbed Jon's sleeve and pointed, "It's Jona!"

Jona had seen them too, and gave a short discreet wave. Jon noticed that she was hiding something under her coveralls.

She got to the group just as they were being swept into a partition.

"We were so worried about you. What happened? Are you OK?" Anie whispered.

"I'm OK. It's a long story – let's go get something to eat first?" she said.

"That's what we were thinking," said Jon.

"Where's Deemus?" Jona asked.

"Who cares?" said Anie angrily.

Jon shrugged. "We haven't seen him since this morning. He appeared... embarrassed about your, ah, meeting with the Warden," he said.

"So he knew?" asked Jona.

"I don't know," said Jon. "He said he knew this had happened before to others."

Jon lowered his voice. "Can you and Anie, um, 'help', her at the appropriate time?" He discreetly pointed to Kiala, who was staring at nothing.

"Now," said Jon, and he dragged Tem backward and stiff-armed him backward over the wall. Jona and Anie each grabbed one of Kiala's arms, and flipped her over as well. They all landed ungracefully but unhurt on the other side.

Jon was afraid that Tem and Kiala would complain, perhaps loudly, about this unexpected detour, but they just looked around, confused but quiet.

Jon helped Jona up. "Are you really all right?"

She smiled weakly, "Been better, but I'm OK. Tired. Hungry."

Jon said, "I think we can do something about the 'hungry' part."

They began walking toward the kitchen.

"Food?" asked Tem.

"Yes, food," said Jon.

Tem and Kiala followed them obediently.

Jona said, "We've got to leave soon."

"Leave?" asked Anie. "And go where?"

"Like Deemus said, 'Down is Out.'"

Now that they had some breathing room, Jon asked, "What happened to you?"

"Oh, I met our warden, really creepy guy, and some of his creepy assistants, and they figured out that I was unpacified, so they pacified me – almost – and I escaped, and stole a lot of really cool stuff, but the warden will be waking up any minute now if he hasn't already, and when he does, he will not be in a good mood. I am so tired."

"He pacified you?" asked Jon, suddenly on his guard.

"Don't look at me like that, I'm fine. I found some stimulant pills and took some, but I think they're wearing off now."

They reached the first locked door, and despite her weariness, Jona had the door unlocked in few seconds.

Jon said, "Hold on, let me check the corridor."

Jona pulled the data tablet out of her bag. "Wait a minute, I'll do it." She whispered a few commands to the camera program. "The coast is clear."

"What is that?" asked Anie.

"A present from the warden." Jona handed the tablet to Jon, who examined it approvingly.

"You have the Warden's codes, too?" He handed the tablet back to Jona.

"Of course. You forget what line of business I'm in."

Jon frowned and said, "Used to be in."

They got to the kitchen without further incident. Jon locked and secured the door with a steel rod and Anie began handing out food trays.

Jona slumped down on a bench by the wall.

Anie heated trays for Tem and Kiala, and they placidly ate.

Jona pointed to them and said, "Good news about that pacification drug. I found some documentation that it has a half-life of two days, so if we can hold out that long, I think the zombie twins will begin to come out of it."

Jon said, "That's good news. For you too."

"Yeah, I'm not feeling so good right now. All I want to do is sleep."

Anie said, "Here, eat something first." She handed Jona some soup.

They all dug into the food. For several minutes, the only sounds anybody made were the sounds of eating and drinking.

Jona reached into her bag and pulled out the vial of stimulant pills and gave it to Jon. "These may come in handy to get those two on their feet when the time comes."

Jon examined the vial and said, "Thanks, you can hold on to them. I don't have any pockets. What else do you have in that bag of tricks?"

She took the tablet back out and said, "It might be a good idea if you learn how to drive this too. Have a seat."

He said, "I'm familiar with that kind of device. You forget what line of business I'm in. But a refresher wouldn't hurt."

He sat down beside her, and she showed him how to query and manipulate the camera programs.

"And you added our names to the 'Do not keep track of' list?"

"Yep," she said, still pleased with herself.

"Do you think you could also remove some names from that list?"

"What do you mean?" she asked.

"Well, wouldn't it be helpful to know what the warden and his security team were doing right now?"

She smacked her head with her hand. "Why didn't I think of that?"

"Don't be too tough on yourself; you've had a hard day."

She grunted. "You can say that again."

They opened the master list and noted the names, but when Jona attempted to delete a name from the list, the computer informed her that names could not be deleted without access permission from both the warden and director of security. Jona tried to hack around the restrictions but got nowhere.

Eventually, she gave up and said, "It was a good idea."

Jon looked at the other crystals in her bag. "What else you got?"

"Some are encrypted and I haven't had time to figure out how to read them."

She picked up a blue crystal, "This one has some pretty interesting stuff. You remember Deemus saying that this place was built on top of another underground city, experimental something, geothermal something?"

"Yeah, I think."

"Well, he was right. Underneath the prison lies an almost fully functional geothermal station, with shafts extending down to the molten core of the planet."

"What?"

"I have no idea how such a massive public works project like that managed to stay a secret. For that matter I don't know how this prison stayed a secret.

"According to the records on the crystal, the geothermal station was only a few months from being fully operational, able to provide virtually limitless power to the Imperium for centuries to come.

"The project was cancelled a little over six years ago by a junior Civil Stability bureaucrat, citing safety and health issues."

"Let me guess, the bureaucrat's initials are MM."

"You got it."

Jon said, "But why shut something like that down? Abundant cheap power would have meant an economic boom for the Imperium."

"And a loss of control for certain members," Jona answered. "I don't think Medusa Mercantus intended to kill the project completely. I think she probably wanted to put it on hold until she could consolidate her power." She closed her eyes.

"Jon I have to sleep now, just for a little bit."

"OK."

They cleaned off the table, and Jona lay down. Jon found some tablecloths, folded one into a pillow and spread the other over her as a blanket.

"It's not much, but..." he began.

"It's fine", she said softly, and was fast asleep.

Anie came over and said softly, "What do we do now?"

Jon looked over at the sleeping Jona. "Let's all try to get some sleep, and then we go."

"Go where?"

"Down is Out."

Frowning at Jon, Anie went over to Tem and Kiala, took their empty trays and said, "It's time to sleep, OK?"

"OK", they said, and Kiala climbed up on the table and lay down. Tem stretched out on the bench below.

Anie and Jon did the same on the next table.

A loud crash startled them all awake. Someone was trying to break in.

Tem and Kiala sat up, looking confused.

Jon hurried over to Jona and grabbed her bag. He pulled out the stimulant tabs and poured out four pills into Anie's hand. "Give them two each."

Jon helped Jona to a sitting position. "How do you feel?"

"Awful." She coughed, stood up and shook her arms and legs. "At least everything's still working."

"Need another tab?" he asked.

She shook her head. "I'm at my limit. I'll be OK."

A thin line of red sparks crept across the top of the door.

"They're cutting their way in. Let's go."

As they left the kitchen, Jon jammed the door lock behind them.

"This should buy us a little more time," he said.

They hurried back toward the opening to the Labyrinth.

They got to the warehouse minutes later, and hurried to the passageway entrance. The passageway itself was dark as night.

Jon asked Jona, "Did I see a lightwand in your bag?"

She handed it to him, and Jon switched it on.

"Everybody ready?" Jon asked.

"This is a trick question, right?" Anie said.

The group descended into the dim passageway.

94

Jona reached out and touched the damp walls. "I don't like this at all." The passageway spiraled downward into the gloom.

Jon said, "We don't have any other options. Let's keep moving."

They moved as fast as they could, pausing only long enough to listen for any sign they were being followed. The only sounds they heard was dripping water and their own labored breathing.

After what seemed an hour, they came upon a rather large dimly-lit chamber, half-full of scattered crates and debris.

Jon said, "Let's rest here for awhile."

"I wonder what this was?" said Jona.

Jon examined one of the opened crates. "Don't know."

Anie said, "I wonder how far away we are from the Labyrinth?"

A voice from the darkness said, "Not as far as you might think."

Everyone jumped up, except Tem and Kiala who sat placidly on a broken crate.

Jon picked up a broken shelf and demanded, "Who are you?"

Out of the shadows walked four men – two armed guards, Warden Dakol, and a man none of them had ever seen.

"I'm Director of Security Kint Almos, and this is the warden of this section, Lar Dakol."

Dakol didn't look happy at all.

The Director looked around at the debris, flicked some dirt off his tunic, and said, "I'm sorry, but I just can't have prisoners escaping on my watch. It looks bad on all kinds of reports. Doesn't it Warden?"

"You've captured them, the matter is closed," Dakol said tightly.

"I don't think so, but we'll discuss that at another time. Now." He gestured to the guards.

The guards approached the group, took Jona's bag from her, and searched each person for hidden weapons.

The guards nodded to the Director.

"Good, now that's out of the way, will you follow me please?" He walked toward another passageway hidden in the shadows. They were led to an elevator, which took them back, of all places, to the Administrative building.

When Jona saw where they were, she groaned, and Jon saw Dakol smile briefly.

They were lead into a high-ceilinged room.

The Director spoke briefly to the Warden, who then left the room without looking back.

"I want you to know, especially you Ms. Altsul, that I am aware of Dakol's, er, shall we say 'interviewing techniques,' and I disapprove of them. However, I have no jurisdiction over his personal actions."

"But," he continued as if he were lecturing a classroom of students, "when he allows a group of people to attempt an escape, well, I do have jurisdiction over that."

"You see, I am sympathetic to your plight."

"You're going to release us?" Anie asked hopefully.

The Director smiled and said, "Oh, no."

"I have to say though that I was very impressed with your ingenuity, especially yours, Ms. Altsul. Even as I speak, our programmers are fixing that security weakness in our surveillance program that you so adroitly exploited."

Jona sullenly started at her feet.

"What happens now?" asked Jon.

"Well, protocol dictates that I send you to the Labyrinth."

"What?" spluttered Jona. "If you were just going to..."

The Director laughed and said, "I had to catch you first, my dear. I told you, it's all about staying off the wrong reports."

"Honestly," the Director continued, "I don't see the down side on this one. You were heading towards the Labyrinth anyway, when you all wake up, you'll be there."

Jona said, "You could give me back my bag."

The Director smiled and covered his nose and mouth with a small mask.

Just then, Jon smelled a garlicky smell, and his vision swam. *I'm really getting tired of this*, was his last thought before he passed out.

Chapter 11

They awoke in a row of beds in a long, dark room.

Jon rubbed his face and looked around.

"Where are we?" croaked Jona.

"Don't know," answered Jon. "Some kind of dormitory, maybe?"

In the dimness outside he could see that the building was surrounded by high walls.

"Is everyone OK?" he asked.

To Jon's surprise and pleasure, Tem said, "My head hurts. Where are we?"

Both Tem and Kiala were still under the influence of the pacification drug, but it was encouraging that they were showing signs of returning to normal.

Jona said, "I wish they hadn't taken away my tablet. But," she said brightly, we still have this." She held out a data crystal.

Jon said, "How did you hide...don't tell me, I don't want to know."

He got up and moved toward the window.

"OK, if no one's hurt, the first order of business is to find a portable light source or some way to make one. The second order of business is protection – weapons. Deemus said there may be unfriendly natives down here so we'll try to stay out of their way, but we need to be able to defend ourselves if necessary."

"Third is sustenance – food and water."

Anie said, "Can't we just stay here? This place seems pretty safe."

"I don't think so. I'd guess that the Director uses this place as a drop-off for people he sends to the Labyrinth. If he needs to send another group, he'll move us along – or worse."

"Also, if there are natives down here, they also must know that this is a drop-off point for new arrivals, unprepared, unarmed..." He let the thought trail off.

Suddenly the room didn't seem so safe.

"OK, we've got a plan, let's get moving," said Jona.

Before they left the dormitory, they looked through cabinets and storage lockers for anything that might be useful. To their surprise, they found several items, including three satchels, and two working lightwands.

They didn't find anything that could be useful as a weapon.

The fact that they did find useful items bothered Jon. If this was indeed a drop-off point, wouldn't earlier groups have found these items?

Slowly, Jon walked out of the dormitory and scanned the immediate area.

The high walls that enclosed them left them with only two options: they could follow the wall parallel to the side of the chamber, or they could follow the wall that led away from the chamber wall, which also sloped slightly downhill.

"Which way?" asked Anie.

Jon and Jona said in unison, "Down is Out."

As they walked past buildings unused for years, Jona asked, "Does anybody have any feel for what time it is?"

Anie said, "I was just wondering that myself."

Jon said, "To me, it feels like mid-morning, but I have no idea how long we were unconscious."

He continued, "One thing is for certain – whether we find any weapons or not, we need to find water soon."

They walked for another several hours in the perpetual dimness. Tem found some broken railings that would provide some protection – unless the natives had projectile or beam weapons.

Jona said, "We need to start looking harder for some water. I know I'm not supposed to think about being thirsty, but it's all I can think about now."

Anie said, "There, you've done it, now I'm thirsty, too."

Jon said, "OK, everybody, let's not get carried away. Agreed, let's focus on water hunting."

Most of the buildings they had passed had been broken into, which worried Jon, but since their arrival, they had not seen or heard anyone or anything.

Up ahead was a cube-shaped, gray, windowless building. Its single door looked as if multiple attempts had been made to open it, but none had been successful.

Tem looked at the building. "A secure warehouse?"

Jon nodded, "So it would seem. Jona?"

She smirked. "Yes?"

"Would you care to use your considerable talents in your, ah, area of expertise?"

"How many data thieves have you put away in your time?"

"Jona, this isn't the time. We need to work together."

She looked at him for several seconds.

"Right. Let me take a look."

She approached the door slowly, studying it like a painter faced with a fresh canvas. Somebody had definitely tried to get in before, apparently by using brute force. The casing on the keypad was severely dented, but the keypad still responded. She pondered the design for several minutes – she guessed that the batteries supplying power to the door were either dead or too weak to power the keypad. If that was the case, when the lock finally lost power, the combination would default to its initial setting. Different manufacturers had different initial settings.

She took a step back from the door. "I'm betting that this is an Integrated Securty Dynamics midline model, and IDS always used all nines as their initial setting. So here goes."

She pressed the '9' key seven times and stepped back. The lock status light changed from red to green, followed by a loud click.

Looking totally pleased with herself, Jona bowed toward the door.

"After you."

Jon put his hand on the handle, then paused and said, "Stay quiet and alert. Just because this door was locked doesn't mean that the place is empty."

The entranceway was illuminated by a very dim red light, but it was enough to see by.

As soon as they were all in, Jon said, "Jona, lock the door again."

"Good idea, I'll also change the code."

"Tell us what it is." said Anie. "We all need to know."

Jona frowned. "All right – 0112358."

Anie smiled and said, "Ah, a Fibonacci sequence."

"How did you know that?" Jona stammered.

"I had a good math teacher. She told me one day I'd be glad I learned it. She was right. Let's go see where we are."

The building was indeed some kind of warehouse. Cubes on each side of the entranceway contained storage cabinets.

Jona looked around and said softly, "The good news is that whatever is in here appears to have been left alone."

Kiala went over to one of the desk systems against the wall and tried to turn it on. No power.

"Jona, I wonder if we can find some long-storage batteries so we can get into their inventory system. That might save some time."

Jon said, "That's an excellent idea." Against all the bad luck they had been having, the return of Tem and Kiala was a welcome sight.

Tem found a locker containing several varieties of power supplies and additional emergency lights.

He handed Kiala two batteries. "I think these might do the trick."

"Um," Kiala said, "I just push the buttons..."

Chuckling, Jona said, "OK, I'll do it."

She took the batteries from her, popped open the power bay, installed the batteries, and started up the computer.

"There you go."

Kiala opened the master inventory database, and scanned the records.

"It seems that this was some kind of medical research laboratory warehouse. There are listed various chemicals in bulk quantities, lab glassware, diagnostic equipment, tomography units... Ah, and several hundred liters of distilled water."

"Excellent. Just what we need."

"And, some dehydrated meals. I don't know how they'll be after..." she scanned the database again, "six years, but we can go have a look."

Jon asked, "Any other items we can use, any security equipment?"

Kiala delved further into the database, "Not that I can see, wait a minute, there are several cases of low power PPDs."

"All right. Let's go find them."

As they made their way through the warehouse, they found stores of distilled water, edible food, portable data tablets, PPDs – Personal Protection Devices, weapons capable of a rendering a person unconscious from a short distance – not a good choice for a long range weapon, but very much better than a stick.

They discovered several cubicles with cots. a kitchen area, and toilets.

Tem said, "I think we should check out the rest of the building and stay here for the night."

"Absolutely," said Jona, flopping down on the nearest cot.

"This is like a luxury hotel."

Jon said, "Yeah, this does seem to be a good place to rest and regroup. Come on Tem, let's go explore the rest of the place. I don't want to be surprised in the middle of the night."

They thoroughly searched the remaining floors for any hidden means to either get in or out, and didn't find any.

As they sat around the table in the kitchen area, Kiala and Anie handed out trays of food.

Jon said, "I'll take the first watch. I'm not taking any chances."

Tem said between huge bites of a chicken casserole, "Fine with me. You know, this has been the best day we've had since we were thrown into this desolate place."

"Here, here," said Kiala, and they knocked their cups together in a toast.

"Yeah, let's rest while we can," said Jon. "You know, this casserole isn't half bad."

Wiping his mouth, Tem said, "Yeah, but I kind of miss that meatloaf."

Kiala kicked him under the table. "Ouch, I'm just kidding."

They all laughed and continued eating.

After everyone had washed and gone to bed, Jon sat by the kitchen entrance, nursing a cup of hot tea.

Jona emerged from the sleeping room and headed for the kitchen. "That tea smells good. Is there any more?" she asked.

"It's on the counter," he said.

From the kitchen, she asked, "Did you find any lemon?"

"No."

"Sugar?"

"On the middle shelf."

"I see it"

A few minutes later she came out and sat down beside him, steaming cup of tea in hand.

"Penny for your thoughts?" she asked.

"Aren't you supposed to be sleeping?" he said.

"Can't help it, I'm a night person."

"Down here, it's always night," he pointed out.

"Right." She sipped her tea. So, penny for your thoughts?"

"You're persistent, aren't you?"

"It helps in my line of work."

He frowned. "I wish you wouldn't keep bringing that up."

She smiled, "Sorry, sometimes I just like to tweak you."

"I noticed."

They sat in silence.

After a while, she asked again, "Penny for your thoughts?"

This time, he laughed, "OK, I give up. I was thinking about how lucky we've been so far. Nobody's been hurt..."

"Speak for yourself, buddy," she corrected him.

"I mean badly, permanently. We're all still here. You know what I mean."

"Right."

"And this place here, I mean, how much safer and catered to could we be?"

"Well, actually, I didn't see any massage tables anywhere."

"Besides that..."

She looked at him. "You think we're being set up?"

He put his empty cup down. "I don't see how, but I have this nagging feeling that things have been a little too easy."

She spluttered, "Too easy? Listen buster..."

He put up his hands, "Sorry; I meant easy for us, you've definitely had the hardest time and done the best."

Now feeling a little awkward, she said, "I just meant that..."

"It's OK."

"Are you married?" she asked suddenly.

He looked away. "Yes," he said softly.

"What's her name?"

"Lara."

"Do you think that Mercantus caught her too?"

He said, "I don't think so. I gave her as much warning as I could, and she's a smart girl."

He looked down. "I miss her," he said softly.

Clearing his throat, Jon asked, "How about you?"

Jona said, "How about me what?"

"Married?"

She snorted, "Are you kidding, I'm a data thief."

"Boyfriend, Significant Other?" he persisted.

In a smaller voice, she said, "No."

"Well, then, there are a lot of single idiots out there."

She laughed. "Thank you, and yes there are."

"Think you can handle the next watch?"

"No problem – go get some sleep."

Chapter 12

The night passed without incident, and the group gathered in the kitchen for breakfast.

Helping himself to seconds on the pancakes, Tem asked, "What's the plan today, Captain?"

Jon said, "Pry as much information as we can out of the computers in here. Maybe some of these machines are networked to others elsewhere in the Labyrinth."

"Or maybe even Outside," said Kiala hopefully.

"Maybe, but I'd be happy with a detailed map of this area. We need to find out where the entrance to the geothermal plant is."

Kiala said, "I'll go back to the inventory computer we found last night, and see if it can provide any more information."

Jona said, "I'll come with you. I think there might have been some portables back in there somewhere."

Jon looked at Tem and said, "How would you like a crash course in weapons modification?"

"The PPDs?"

"Yeah, let me show you how to turn a low-power device into a high-power device."

"Cool, let's go," said Tem.

"I'm coming too." said Anie.

They went down to the basement where they had found several cases of PPDs the night before. Jon opened a case and laid three of them on a worktable.

"Now, the aim of this exercise is to increase the range of the device. Ordinarily, a low-power PPD is effective only at a distance of about ten feet. After that, the assailant just gets a pin-prickly feeling, really unpleasant, but definitely not incapacitating."

Anie asked, "Are you speaking from experience, or a textbook?"

"Experience," Jon said, and winced at the memory. "During training, we all had to take one hit from a PPD at point-blank, and one hit at 15 feet. I wouldn't recommend trying it at home."

He picked up a PPD.

"OK, we're going to take the parts of two of these low-power devices and put them together. That should give us a weapon with a range of thirty to forty feet. The enhanced range does come at a cost though – the effective number of uses drops to about 3, but it looks like we have enough spare power supplies that we can make quite a few. We should be all right, unless we get in a firefight with somebody with superior firepower."

"Then we're toast anyway," said Tem.

"All we can do is prepare the best we can," said Anie.

"That's the attitude," said Jon. He flicked open the access panel of the PPD. "First thing we do is remove the power source and baffle. The baffle is what spreads the charge across a wide area so you don't have to aim precisely."

"With our modification, we do want to be able to aim, so we're going to make the baffle into a cone, like this."

He twisted the baffle around his finger into a cone shape, and reinserted it into the PPD.

"The second thing we need to do is to fit additional power sources on to the handle."

Tem said, "Wouldn't you just connect them in series?"

Pleased, Jon said, "That's correct. How did you know that?"

Tem said, "I used to play Lightball. We would, um, enhance, our weapons. When we could get away with it."

Jon asked, "Were you a good shot?"

"At forty feet? Oh yeah."

Jon took a power source out of the second PPD and attached it to the bottom of the PPD's own power source. He then took some self-molding plastic, and extended the pistol grip over the second power source.

"It looks awkward, but it works."

———————

Jona and Kiala scoured through several databases they had found on the inventory computer.

"Look at this," said Kiala excitedly. "It looks like a map of this place."

Jona said, "According to this, all we need to do is follow the main street downward, and we should be at the top level of the main part of the geothermal plant."

Kiala pointed to a dark corridor along the main street. "What's this?"

Jona studied it for a second, then said, "Don't know. Maybe some temporary construction. No big deal. After all, we've got lights, and the boys and

Anie are making weapons. Plus, since we've been here we haven't seen a soul."

Kiala shivered. "Yeah, that's what scares me."

"Come on, let's download this into our tablets and see what other stuff we can find."

They spent the rest of the day plundering among the cabinets and containers.

That night, the two groups compared notes.

Looking at the map, Jon pointed to the entrance to the geothermal station. "This is where we need to go," he said.

"But what about the security?" asked Jona.

"What if the elevators aren't working?" asked Kiala.

"What about..." Tem began.

Jon held up his hands. "Hold on; let's take it one step at a time. We've dealt with plenty to get here; we'll deal with what we find when we get there."

Kiala said, "Why can't we go out in the morning and do some more reconnaissance, check the place out. We should easily be able to get there and back in a day."

"You want to come back here?" Jon said.

"Why not?" said Anie. We're safe here."

Jona added, "We have shelter, sustenance, and security – at least so far. And I don't know about anyone else, but I could use a day or two more of regular meals and sleeping in a real bed."

Jon thought for a moment.

OK, you sold me. We go out and look around tomorrow, come back and plan our next moves."

They went to bed early that night. Jon scattered some infrared alarms around the perimeter of their sleeping area. Unless they were dealing with professionals, they would be safe.

As soon as Jon's head hit the pillow, he was fast asleep.

He was home, in the kitchen, sitting at the table, and watching Lara make muffins. She always made blueberry muffins from scratch. She mixed the batter carefully, dropping the blueberries in at just the right time, and placing big dollops of the mixture into the muffin trays.

He loved the way the house smelled when she baked...

Lara was telling him something. She put the mixing bowl down and seemed upset about something. He looked over at the oven, and there stood Medusa Mercantus wearing oven mitts, holding the half-baked tray of muffins. Lara was crying, and Medusa left carrying the tray of muffins.

Over her shoulder, Medusa winked at him and called out, "Timing is everything."

Jon woke to a strange, rhythmic hollow sound. He quickly grabbed one of the enhanced PPDs they made the day before, and headed back toward the source of the sound. Tem was right behind him.

"What's going on?" asked Jona.

Pausing in the doorway, Jon said, "Stay here and have a PPD ready. Be ready to use it, but check your target before you fire – don't shoot us."

"Right," she said.

They followed the sound to the top floor in the back of the warehouse. There were no signs of forced entry and the sound seemed to be coming from the roof.

Tem listened intently. "Man, animal, or machine?" he wondered.

Jon said, "It can't be the wind. If we could just see outside..."

"Wait a minute, I wonder if this place has external security cameras," said Tem.

"I didn't see any around front, but we didn't go all the way around the outside of the building. Let's go find out."

They returned to the sleeping area, making sure that they announced themselves loudly as they walked into the kitchen.

Frowning, Jona lowered her PPD. "Aw, man, I was looking forward to shooting somebody. Come on Jon, let me wing you."

"No, put that away," he ordered with mock alarm.

"You're no fun. What was making that noise?"

"We don't know. It seemed to be coming from the roof." He listened. "It's stopped."

Kiala said, "Yeah, about five minutes ago."

Tem said, "Jona, did you see any surveillance controllers in any of the computers you looked at yesterday."

"No. I would have told you."

"Whatever or whoever it was seems to be gone now. We're already up, so let's eat breakfast and get ready to move out."

As they ate – rehydrated oatmeal with cinnamon – Jon said, "Let's split up into two groups; one group will stay here and hold down the fort, and the other will go investigate the geothermal station."

"OK," said Kiala doubtfully.

"Fine with me," Jona shrugged. "Who goes and who stays?"

Jon said, "Well, since you mentioned it, and don't take this personally, but maybe you could use some more rest."

Jona grinned and said, "Oh, no offense taken. Actually I wanted to investigate something I'd need to be here to do anyway."

Jon asked, "And that would be..."

"Once upon a time, the computers in this warehouse were part of a much larger network. I want to see if I can talk to any of the other computers on the network. Who knows what I could find, more maps, elevator control programs, communications facilities..."

"That'd be great. All right, stay here and hack."

"Anie, if you want, you can stay here too. You were pretty sick from the toxic reaction to the pacification drug."

"Thanks. I could use another day of not being scared all the time."

"OK, then, the three of us will head out."

Jona handed them three data tablets. "I downloaded the maps we found into these tablets. You should be able to navigate with no problems."

"Lock the door behind us."

Jon went outside and cautiously checked all around the building. There was nothing that wasn't there the day before.

Jona said, "Remember the password. Otherwise, I shoot."

"Understood."

"Be careful and come back safe."

"Job Number One."

As they walked toward the geothermal station, Kiala asked, "What's the password again?"

Tem said, "I thought you knew."

"It's going to be a long day," Jon muttered as the two giggled.

'Day' was an arbitrary term down here. The faint glow from almost-dead phosphorescent streetlights and building signs provided the only illumination, apart from their lightwands. More than once, Kiala thought she saw movement in one of the deserted buildings, but the image turned out to be just a lightwand beam reflected in some broken glass.

Some time earlier, there had been a rockfall, and some of the buildings along the side had been smashed in.

The whole scene was desolate and depressing, and they all found themselves wishing they could locate the geothermal station, so they could get back to the comfort and safety of the warehouse.

Around mid-morning, Jon said, "Break time. Let's move over to the entranceway to that building. I want to be out of sight of the main road."

Ten asked, "You think somebody is following us?"

"No, but we need to be as unobtrusive as possible."

Kiala asked, "How much farther?"

Jon consulted his tablet. "We're coming to the end of this chamber. We go through the tunnel ahead, and from there it looks like another two miles or so, and we should be there."

Kiala said, "Good, this place gives me the creeps."

Jon said, "Me too. OK, let's go. The sooner we get there the sooner we get back."

They headed toward the tunnel indicated on the map.

Looking to the right and left of the chamber wall, Tem saw dozens of similar tunnels.

In a few minutes, they stood in front of the tunnel that led to the station. They could see no light coming from the other side.

"It probably bends in the middle," Tem said hopefully.

"Or it's caved in," Kiala responded.

"Only one way to find out," Jon said. "OK, everybody ready?"

"Like we have a choice," Kiala said."

"That's the spirit."

They walked briskly into the tunnel, feet slapping shallow pools of water formed from the damp ceilings and walls.

Soon, the tunnel entrance was a small circle of dim light behind them. As Tem had speculated, the tunnel bent to the right, but they could still not see any sign of light ahead.

After they had walked another few minutes, Kiala looked back and saw a brief flash of light. She gasped, and the others immediately stopped.

"What is it?" asked Jon.

"I saw a light," said Kiala.

"Are you sure?" asked Tem.

"I'm sure," she snapped.

"Maybe it was a reflection in a puddle or something?"

"I know what I saw."

Just then, they heard rustling sounds coming from both directions.

Kiala whispered, "Did you hear that?"

"Yes," whispered both Jon and Tem.

Jon reached into his pack and pulled out his PPD.

"We're probably closer to the far end of the tunnel, so let's keep moving, and get your PPDs ready," he whispered.

Suddenly, black shapes sprang from the walls around them. Jon got off a shot from his PPD, but he had fired at such close range, the charge had spread in the narrow confines of the tunnel. He felt his legs go weak, and he slid to the ground.

"Kiala? Tem? Are you OK?" he said in a strangled voice. There was no answer.

He guessed that he had probably stunned his assailants, but before he could recover and get to his feet, he felt more hands take the weapon from him. Someone grabbed his neck, and he felt a sharp prick, then he felt nothing.

Chapter 13

He ran straight up smooth tunnels in the Labyrinth. He didn't feel tired. He didn't feel afraid. He felt strong, happy, free. He ran up the side of a sheer cliff, and shouted with joy. He looked back at Jona, and Tem, and Kiala, and Anie, and Deemus was there too, looking bemused in a crazy kind of way. He ran, higher and higher. Soon he would be at the ceiling, and he wondered, no, he knew, that he could run on the ceiling, over the heads of all those people below.

He got to the point where the wall met the ceiling, and he jumped onto the ceiling, but instead of running, he started falling, He felt sick as the ground rushed up to meet him. He closed his eyes, and when he opened them, he was rushing toward water, about to hit. He closed his eyes again and held his breath, then he felt the stinging slap of the impact followed by the cold bubbles rising around him.

He swam up toward the surface, but when he emerged, gasping for air, he found himself on the ceiling again, falling back toward the water.

———

He woke up, and the first thing he felt was a hand against his face. After a moment of panic, he realized his arm must have gone to sleep, because when he touched it with his other arm, it felt cold and detached. He sat up, wide awake, rubbing his arm to try to get some sensation back. He could see nothing. Total darkness. He called out tentatively, "Kiala? Tem?" Several feet to his right, he heard a soft moan.

"Kiala? Is that you?"

"Yeah, I suppose. What happened? Where are we?"

"Don't know. I'm OK, are you OK?"

"I feel a little numb. Whatever they used must have had some local anesthetic in it."

Several feet beyond Kiala, Tem groaned.

"Tem, are you OK?"

"Neck hurts, can't see anything. Hungry, thirsty, just been captured by who-knows-who, and lying in total darkness several miles underneath the surface of the planet." He coughed. "Other than that, I'm good."

Jon said, "I'm really getting tired of waking up on cold hard floors."

Kiala said, "You forgot damp. I'm in a puddle."

Above them, a light appeared. The intensity of it temporarily blinded them, and they shielded their eyes.

An unnaturally deep voice said, "Good, you're awake. I go tell the King."

The light stopped and they were again in darkness. Jon blinked back the retinal ghosts.

Tem said, "Did he just say, 'I go tell the King?'"

Kiala said, "That's what it sounded like."

They waited.

"So that's what getting shot by a PPD feels like," said Kiala.

Jon snorted. "Kind of. A direct hit is a lot more intense. You don't have time for your legs to go wobbly – one second you're standing up, the next you're face down on the ground, wondering how you got there."

"Thank goodness we didn't get a direct hit," said Tem

"I wonder what this King is like," said Kiala.

"I have a feeling we're going to meet him soon enough."

They waited.

———————

After what felt like an hour, a door above opened and three packages were thrown down. This time, the light wasn't so intense, and Jon quickly surveyed their confinement. In the corner was a lavatory and toilet.

The packages contained blankets, food bars, water containers, toilet paper, and a small personal biolight.

"I guess they intend for us to stay awhile," said Kiala.

The overhead door was still open, and Jon shouted, "Hello. Can we talk to you?" He heard the sounds of several people whispering, but no one answered.

After a few minutes the door closed again, leaving them in darkness.

"Do we want to light one of our biolights?"

Well, we have three, and we do need to see to get to the toilet."

"Yes, please," said Kiala.

Jon activated his, and it glowed a dull green, sufficient to cast a ghostly pall on them all.

They ate their food bars and drank the water in silence.

After they finished their meal, Kiala asked, "Now what?"

"Whoever this King is he's obviously in no hurry to see us, so let's just conserve our energy until our situation changes."

Jon yawned and said, "I'll take the first watch."

Kiala said, "Oh, just go to sleep. We're prisoners, so what does it matter if you know somebody's coming after you a millisecond early?"

"I guess you're right."

They all slept.

The door overhead opened and a voice called out, "Wakey, wakey." A brilliant light shone down on them, and a rope ladder was lowered down.

"Come up; the lady first."

Kiala shrugged, and climbed up the ladder, disappearing into the bright light.

Next Tem went up, followed by Jon.

They found themselves in a mirrored chamber, with a single powerful light focused down into the chamber they had just climbed out of.

In front of them stood a short albino man. He blinked at them, then said, "It's time to go meet the King. Follow me." He moved off toward a hidden doorway in the mirrored wall. They followed.

Jon said, "Could you answer some questions? Who are you? Where are we?"

The albino looked back and placidly said, "The King will answer any questions if he feels you need to know."

"Who is the King?" asked Kiala.

"He might answer that one."

———————

They followed the guide through a vast maze of hollowed out rooms and interconnecting tunnels. Some of the tunnels were so small they all had to crouch. At one point, Jon had to get on his hands and knees to keep going.

Jon tried to memorize the twists and turns they were taking, but finally had to give up—there was no way to keep track of all the turns they had made.

Eventually, the group came to a rather large chamber, which appeared to be a waiting or reception area. Jon was surprised to see an ancient bookcase filled with well-used books.

"Do you think we'll be able to find our way back?" whispered Kiala.

"No," answered Jon. "I tried keeping track, but it wouldn't do any good anyway. I don't have any point of reference. It wouldn't do us much good to go back to that dungeon."

The guide indicated chairs against the wall, and said, "Sit. His Majesty will see you shortly." He left the room through a side door.

Trying to lighten the mood, Tem said, "I've never met royalty before, I wonder how we should address him?"

Jon said, "Just be careful about saying anything. Who knows, this person may be as loony as Deemus."

"For all we know, he may *be* Deemus," Kiala said.

Tem said, "In that case, I'm sorry we parted on such bad terms."

The side door opened again, and a rather large woman swept in and approached them.

Without introduction or preamble, she began, "Pay attention! You must always address the King as 'Your Majesty.' Also – do not speak unless spoken to."

Tem asked, "What happens if we break these rules?"

The woman fixed him with a cold stare and said, "You don't want to find out, do you?"

Tem looked down at his feet.

Jon said, "Well, can we ask you some questions?"

"Pertaining to interacting with His Majesty?"

"Among other things."

She looked doubtful but said, "Go ahead."

"Thank you. For starters, where are we?"

She looked confused by the question, "We are in the Kingdom, of course."

"The Kingdom," repeated Jon.

"Yes, the Kingdom of the Labyrinth. As if that weren't perfectly obvious."

"How did you get here?" asked Kiala.

Now the woman really looked confused. "Same as you. From the prison."

Her face darkened. "Threw us away, they did. We'll see who's expendable."

Her bracelet chimed, and she said, "Your audience with the Most Wise King of the Labyrinth is about to begin. Follow me, and remember what I told you." She looked pointedly at Tem.

Wide doors opened at one end of the room, and the woman walked briskly through. As he followed, Jon felt a slight tingle — they were being scanned.

Armed guards blocked their way until the scan turned green, then parted as the woman motioned them to follow her.

They were on a raised platform in a brightly-lit, long room. Boxes and crates were stacked up on each side of the room. All along the room, at regular intervals, were open doorways. People began streaming through; noisy, eager, as if they were anticipating a great entertainment.

As they walked down the center platform, Jon tried to determine the contents of the boxes. Most seemed to be computer and electronic parts. He also saw secure containers of weapons — PPDs, energy rifles, stealth missiles. He wondered what the King was doing with all that firepower.

The King sat on a raised platform at the far end of the room. When they were close enough to make out his features, Kiala gasped. He looked just like Deemus!

"It can't be," she whispered to Jon.

"Take it easy. Just follow our instructions," Jon whispered back.

The King, who could have been the identical twin of the man they had known back at the prison, watched them approach — apparently without recognition. Jon wasn't sure what to make of this. The King was dressed in military fatigues with a black wool cape. He was clean-shaven and his long hair was clean and combed,

"Well, if it is Deemus, he cleaned himself up pretty well," said Kiala quietly.

Glaring at Kiala, the woman stopped and motioned for them to do likewise.

"Your Majesty. Guests desiring to enrich your kingdom."

In a surprisingly deep, rich voice, the King said, "Thank you. You may go." The woman bowed deeply — Tem wondered if she would pitch over forward — and left the room through an entrance that Jon had not noticed.

The King regarded them calmly and said, "Come closer, honored guests."

"Honored guests..." Kiala began, but Tem grabbed her arm and whispered furiously, "Remember what the woman said." Still fuming, she held her tongue.

The King motioned for them to come closer. When they came within ten feet of the throne, guards blocked their way and they stopped.

The King got up from his throne and walked down to the three prisoners. Unlike Deemus, who walked with a limp, the King walked with an easy grace.

"Now, what brings you to our esteemed presence?" he said jovially, as if he were indeed welcoming them as guests.

Both Tem and Kiala started to speak, but Jon said, "We were passing through this area, when we were, ah, detained by your people."

"Detained?" asked the king. An assistant approached him and whispered in his ear. "Ah, yes, you attacked our sentries with some sort of weapon."

Tem blurted out, "We attacked you? Your thugs attacked us!" The King looked at him as if he had not spoken.

He paced back and forth in front of them, looking completely at ease. The guards, who were always one step behind him, looked very capable of disabling or killing anyone who made a threatening move.

"Friends," he began, "I am on a mission. I was once like you, running from those who had enslaved you.

"But I had the fortune of ending up here, and helped by these fine people around me, have begun a quest."

Despite the large woman's warning, Jon asked, "What kind of quest?"

The King said, "An excellent question, sir!"

"My quest." He paused. "Our quest," he spread his arms to include everybody present, "is to free all of our imprisoned subjects trapped in the dark mills above."

In a louder voice, he continued, "I will lead our mighty army to conquer the Overlords who cast us all down into this place. We will drive them up, up into the light of the outside world, and we will take our rightful place as the new leaders."

"Everybody needs a hobby," muttered Tem.

This the King heard, and he rushed past his guards and grabbed Tem by the collar, and bent him backward. For someone who looked as frail as Deemus, he was surprisingly strong. Jon made a move to help, but was stopped by one of the guards.

"We don't appreciate those who would make light of our quest."

"I can see that," said Tem in a strangled voice.

"Let him go," pleaded Kiala. "Please?"

The King looked at her, smiled, and said, "As you wish."

He released Tem, who promptly fell backwards and sat down unceremoniously.

"Thank you." said Kiala.

The King bowed slightly. "It is not my aim to intimidate, but I will not have our quest made light of."

Just to see what would happen, Jon asked, "How can we help?"

The King looked at him with renewed interest and asked, "How, indeed?"

A murmur swept thought the crowd as Jon began to regret his offer.

The King calmly returned to his throne and sat down.

"That's a question worth answering," the King said.

After a moment, the King got to his feet and said in an amplified voice carried throughout the chamber, "My loyal subjects, your toil and patience will soon be rewarded. I salute you!"

A cheer went up from the crowd, and the King raised his fists in a victory gesture. Kiala took advantage of the noise to say, "I don't understand, where did all these people come from? Why were we kept in their prison so long?"

Jon said, "I don't know, but I'm afraid that this isn't over."

As if on cue, the King looked down at them, and Jon could barely hear him say, "Bring them," as he left the room.

Four guards approached them, two behind and two on each side. They were lead to another hidden doorway below the one the King had just gone through.

They now found themselves in another waiting room, but this one was more sparsely furnished, and smelled of antiseptic.

Kiala said, "I have a bad feeling about this."

"Nonsense," said the King from behind them. "As long as you are here, you are under my protection."

"Does that protection include being thrown into a lightless dungeon for over a day?" Tem asked.

This time, the King looked at him mildly. "Our apologies. Your presence was not brought to my attention until this morning."

"Now if you will please step into the four cubicles in front of you..."

Kiala drew back and a guard grabbed her arm.

"Oh, don't worry, you won't be harmed. Think of this as a job interview."

There was nothing to do but cooperate.

The King looked at Jon. "Good, since you're obviously the leader, I'll start with you."

A guard shoved Jon into one of the cubicles, and Jon lay down on a form-fitting couch. Through speakers embedded in the couch, Jon heard the voice of the King, unnaturally resonant, "Now, please lie back and relax."

As Jon did so, restraints closed around his neck, arms, chest, and legs. He tensed, expecting the worst.

"Please relax. The restraints are there for your own protection. We're going to administer a mild sedative and muscle relaxant." Jon felt a small prick on the inside of his left arm.

"Most subjects find this pleasant. Rest assured; this is not torture. We're merely preparing you for the interview."

"What, what interview?" Jon slurred. He was already getting sleepy. The King was right – his unease had been replaced by a growing euphoria.

"We need to determine how you can help my army – what skills and talents you have that we can use."

Now Jon felt positively happy. A small corner of his mind knew that this happiness was chemically induced, but he was powerless to resist. And why would anyone resist feeling like this?

A distant voice said, "I think we're ready to begin. What is your name?"

Jon felt that he should try to resist, but he couldn't think why.

"Jon Prospero."

"Now, Jon, tell me about your life before you were taken to the prison."

Jon now found the voice utterly compelling. Was it still the King's voice? He couldn't tell. He just knew that he felt warm and safe, and wanted to be useful.

Over the next hour, Jon, in a sleepy voice, narrated his pre-prison life, his education, training, work for the Imperium. The voice gently probed and prodded, and Jon willingly told it details about his weapons experience and surveillance qualifications.

Finally, he became aware of a rushing sound and bright lights. He sat up in his chair, blinking and disoriented.

A man he had not seen before helped him out of the cubicle. He offered Jon a drink, which Jon gladly accepted.

In the next two cubicles, Kiala and Tem slowly got up from their couches.

In another room adjoining the interview room, the King and two of his advisers pored over the information they had just extracted from Jon, Kiala, and Tem.

An eager young advisor scanned Jon's information excitedly. "Your Majesty, this is truly a gift – an Imperium Investigator, who has weapons and surveillance training. He probably has more military resources that can be tapped!"

The King mused, "Yes, his surveillance experience could be a great asset, although I don't need any additional help planning our campaign." He looked pointedly at the young man. "Do you believe I need help?"

The advisor turned red. "Of course not, Your Majesty."

The King frowned. "What about the other two?"

The older advisor said, "Neither has any significant strategic or tactical experience. The male," he consulted his tablet, "Tem Koltoo, is, was, an academic."

The young advisor interjected, "He was the insolent one."

Irritated, the King replied, "I remember. Thank you."

The older advisor continued, "The female is an accounting specialist. We already have several that match her qualifications fairly closely."

The King said, "Are they worth keeping? For manual labor?"

The older advisor said, "I recommend we keep the group intact, at least for the near term. We definitely want Jon Prospero, but he may have mental conditioning that we would need to defeat, and if we remove his friends, he may react badly."

The King said, "Very well. For now, keep them all together."

"But continue the obedience treatments. I want to know that Prospero is a reliable asset by this time next week."

"Yes, Your Majesty," said his advisors in unison.

Guards led the three prisoners to a different, slightly larger cell, containing four cots.

As the door closed behind them, Tem said, "I'm so sleepy," and fell into the nearest cot.

As she took the next cot, Kiala said, "I can't think, and I'm too tired to care."

Jon grunted and collapsed onto the remaining cot.

He dreamed that he was again in the King's narrow room, but this room had two paths leading to the front. One path sloped downward towards heat and light. As he walked nearer, he could feel the heat against his skin.

The other path lead upward into darkness. The King stood along the upward path, surrounded by his guards and followers. His image flowed and sputtered, like a bad hologram, and Jon heard a noise like a rushing of great winds. The King beckoned him and instinctively Jon turned and hurried down the lower path, despite the growing heat. He looked over to see the King angrily shouting to his followers to pursue Jon, but as they tried to follow him down, their clothes burst into flames from the incredible heat, and their screams of pain were horrible...

Jon sat up in his cot, sweating heavily. He got up and shuffled to the sink. He splashed his face and drank some water. The coolness made him feel a little better, and he went back and lay down on his cot. Staring at the ceiling, he tried to reconstruct what had brought them here. He knew that they had been drugged (again) and that he had held no information back, past or present, so it was a good assumption that some of the King's army would be on their way to apprehend Jona and Anie.

He found himself wanting that sense of wellbeing that the drugs gave him, and wondered if he had already become dependent.

He rolled over and looked at the sleeping forms of Tem and Kiala. He felt his sweat-soaked shirt and wondered if the withdrawal was already starting.

We have to get out of here, he thought with a sudden pang of fear.

Tem rolled over and opened his eyes.

He asked, "What happened to us?"

"Our host administered some kind of hypnotic truth-telling drug and probably asked us lots of questions."

"Why?"

Jon shrugged. "My guess is he's looking for additional personnel for his quest. He was probably probing for military or paramilitary experience."

Tem said, "But he's got to know that we won't cooperate?"

Jon looked at him. "We already have. And the truth serum may well also be an addictive narcotic."

"You mean like the pacification drug we were given before?"

"Similar, but this one promises to be nastier. I'm guessing withdrawal from this drug will really hurt."

"Oh. I wonder what use the King would have with a statistician and an accountant."

Jon didn't say anything.

Kiala quietly said, "We wouldn't have any military value, except to stop bullets."

Tem said, "Oh."

Kiala rubbed her temples. "I don't know if this matters or not, but I'm getting one whopper of a headache."

Tem lay back in his cot. "I feel a little queasy myself. Jon, look on the bright side, at least you're not allergic to this drug."

Jon laughed humorlessly. "Yeah, great."

Just then, the door opened and two hooded figures rolled in a cart with trays.

Tem said, "No thanks, we're not hungry."

The figures flung back their hoods.

"Jona! Anie!"

"Well, it's a good thing you're not hungry, because I couldn't find any untainted food in this rat's maze," said Jona.

Anie asked, "How is everybody?"

"We've been better," said Tem.

Jona said, "Here, take these." She pulled three vials of clear liquid out of her pocket.

Taking a vial, Jon asked, "What is it?"

"It's an antidote for the obedience drug that you were given in your interrogation. It won't prevent all the withdrawal symptoms, but it should lessen the severity. Actually, you're lucky – you only got the initial dose, and this stuff is supposed to work pretty well."

The other two took their vials.

"Down the hatch," said Tem and drank his vial.

Jon said, "We need to get out of here."

Jona laughed and said, "You think?" She opened up a compartment in the cart she had pushed in, and produced three hooded capes. "Here, put these on. Are you all strong enough to travel?"

Kiala said, "We'll have to be."

Tem asked, "How did you find us?"

As she handed out PPDs to everyone, Jona said, "I'll tell you later. For now, keep your faces and PPDs hidden and walk slowly. If anybody stops us, don't say anything, just bow and follow my lead. We'll know if we need to start shooting. Now, let's see if we can figure our way out of here."

Chapter 14

They followed Jona through what seemed miles of twisting tunnels. They met dozens of hooded and robed workers, but no one stopped them. Several times, Jona surreptitiously consulted a map she had hidden in her robes.

Only once did they get a scare. One of the Kings advisors walked past them, staring at them suspiciously. But they kept moving and the advisor eventually turned and continued on his way.

When they were safely out of earshot, Jona whispered, "OK, this is as far as I got with my plan. There's an old tram station up ahead, and the maps I could find indicate that it goes to the geothermal station."

"That's perfect," said Jon.

"Not quite. Some parts are blocked off – we may have to go back up a level or two in order to keep going forward."

Jon said, "I can deal with that."

Jona looked at her tablet.

"There's some other bad news," she said.

"What?"

"We've just been discovered. Time to go."

Consulting her map as they ran, Jona said, "Though here is an access panel leading to the tram tunnel. Somebody open it. Quick."

Jon and Tem wrestled the heavy panel off, revealing a tiny corridor barely big enough to crawl through.

"OK, everybody in. Hurry."

They all scurried in and with an effort, Jon and Tem replaced the panel.

Jona turned on a lightwand. "OK, this way, there's another panel several hundred feet down the line."

"Several hundred feet – my knees," complained Tem.

The group slowly crawled toward the second access panel up ahead. When they got to it, Jona said, "Quiet, listen for voices."

Not daring to breathe, the group listened in silence for several tense minutes.

Jon said, "OK, let's do it."

Once again, Jon and Tem opened the heavy access panel and placed it as quietly as they could against the outer wall.

They crawled out of the accessway, stretching, and rubbing their knees.

Tem looked around and said, "Hey, this is where we need to be! Look."

Up ahead was an open tram tunnel with a sign against the back wall that read 'Destination: Geothermal Station.'

They approached a tram car and examined it.

"Do we want to see if we can get this thing running?" asked Kiala.

Jon said, "I don't think so. It would alert the King to our position. How far is the Geothermal Station from here."

Jona consulted her map. "About six miles – a pretty good hike."

"There are several more tram stops between here and there. Maybe we can get to the first one, and find somewhere to hole up."

"Sounds good to me. By then, we should be ready for a rest."

"I'm ready now," said Tem.

Jon said. "First, let's put some distance between us and the King."

As they moved off at a good pace, Kiala asked Jona, "OK, how did you find us?"

"Right. After y'all left, Anie and I did some old-fashioned cable tracing in some of the rooms at the front of the warehouse, and we found the network server in a closet. So we pull it out, and get it running again, and as it boots up, it tried to reestablish connection with all the computers it knew about before it went down."

"Apparently, one of the systems it communicated with belonged to His Highness back there, and its access credentials were still good, so I snooped around his systems to see what he was up to, and stumbled upon your interrogation record, Jon. Quite an impressive resume.

"Anyway, the system knew where you were being kept, and when your next Interrogation session would be."

Kiala shivered. "It's horrible to think that we would be back there, with these people romping around in our brains."

Jona cleared her throat, then said, "Well, actually Jon was the only one who was going back for a second round. You two were expendable, only to be kept around until they knew they had broken Jon – after that happened, y'all would be carted off and – I didn't pursue how you would have been, what term did they use – 'resolved?'"

Tem let out a deep breath. "But why didn't they kill us right after the interview?"

"Apparently, they thought it would have upset Jon and made him less cooperative."

"And it would have, too," said Jon. "I would have been very put out."

"So anyway," continued Jona, "we headed out as soon as we saw the schedule. Getting in was actually the easy part. Believe it or not, they have something similar to an 'employee entrance' which is virtually unguarded. All you need is the outfit, and the single guard waves you right through."

"What did you learn from my interview?" asked Jon.

Jona shrugged and said, "Stuff every data thief I know would give his or her front temporal lobe for. I have to give you guys credit."

Before he could respond, she said, "Don't worry, if we get out of this, I'm going straight. Maybe I could even be on your team?" she teased.

Jon didn't know whether to believe her or not.

They walked and ran on for another half an hour before arriving at a tram stop. This one seemed to be a hub for other tram lines, and the wallmap indicated food dispensaries and guest quarters.

"Look at this – food and beds – we're in luck!"

"OK, but stay alert. We don't know if our hosts behind us have other means of transportation."

They made their way through the central transportation mall – this stop was indeed a hub connecting four tram lines, and they could see that when this mall had been in use, it must have been a busy place, full of vendors, shops, restaurants, people going in all directions.

Tem said, "I can't imagine how they managed to keep all this secret. From the looks of it, this transportation system could have moved thousands of people around each day."

"If it was at capacity," said Jon. "I don't think it was."

"Still, this is an amazing achievement. And it was just abandoned."

Jon looked around warily. "Let's find some provisions and get out of sight as soon as possible. I don't like walking around like this."

"I think I can eat now," said Tem.

They found an intact food dispensary and filled their packs with self-heating meals.

"Thank goodness for long shelf life," said Kiala as she sorted through different meal choices.

Anie said, "I'm just glad we found some food. Sometimes I feel like we're running blindfolded in the dark."

"Me too," said Jon. "Meatballs?"

"Thank you," said Anie. She took the offered tray and slid it into her pack.

"Where's Tem?" asked Kiala. "I thought he said he was hungry."

"He went down that way," said Jona, pointing to the far end of the concourse. Anie waved at him and said, "Here he comes. Uh oh, he seems to be in a hurry."

They watched as Tem sprinted towards them.

"We've got to leave now," he gasped as he reached them.

"Why?" asked Jon, reaching for his PPD.

"People with guns at the end of the concourse. Heading this way."

"Wonderful," said Jona, putting her boots back on.

"OK, let's go."

"Which way?"

"Back the way we came."

"What? Won't they be following us?"

Jon gritted his teeth. "Probably. I'll take a look."

He ran back toward the tunnel entrance, and as he looked down the tunnel, he could see distant lights and hear footsteps and the sound of metal.

He ran back toward the group.

"We need another plan."

Anie said, "Let's see if we can ride."

They all looked at her. "What?"

She pointed to a darkened hallway underneath a sign that read 'Tram Maintenance Personnel Only.'

Anie said, "Come on." She ran toward the hallway.

"Anie, wait!" called Jon. "Where is she going?"

Jona picked up her pack. "It looks like she's got the plan."

They all followed Anie into the hallway. *At least we can hide here*, Jon thought. Anie examined all the doors down the hallway. Toward the end, she saw what she was looking for – an accessway to a parallel tram tunnel.

She tried to open the door, but it was locked.

"Allow me," said Jona, and stepped up to the lock.

Anie stopped her. "No, I can do this one." She deftly entered a series of numbers and the door slid open, revealing a control room full of lights, meters, and displays.

Amazed, Jon said, "How did you know that this was here?"

"Get in, get in," she said. They all crowded into the small space, and when everybody was inside, she closed the door and scrambled the lock.

Anie said, "That should buy us some time. Those doors are usually riot-proof."

"Anie, how..." began Jona.

"All tram stations have small tunnels running just below the main tram tunnel. Maintenance personnel use them to make minor repairs and add communication capacity without taking tunnel traffic off-line."

"This system runs on a self-contained battery, in case the main system loses power. I hoped it would still be good."

She touched a display showing the entire local grid.

"Look here." She pointed to a green tram line leading back where they had come from. "Your friend the King is sending more people to look for us." She touched several icons in rapid succession. The line now flashed red.

"I've just put that tram line in 'protective maintenance' mode – the ends of the line, which terminate here, and at the station down the line, now have a weak electrical barrier covering the tunnel. If anyone tries to enter the tunnel now, they'll get a weak, but meaningful electric shock, not enough to cause any damage, but enough to persuade anyone not to enter."

She touched several more icons and a hatch opened on the other side of the small chamber. Beyond the hatch was a tube with two reclining seats – one behind the other. Behind the back seat was an empty cargo area.

"The maintenance tram only holds two people, so two of you get in. Once you get out, the tram will automatically return."

"Where can we go?"

Anie beamed. "Right where we want to go – the geothermal station."

Jon said, "OK, I'll go first. Kiala, want to come?"

Looking at the maintenance tram, Kiala said, "I never liked enclosed spaces. Do I have a choice?"

"No, and keep your PPD ready – we don't know what'll be at the other end."

"Wonderful."

Anie said, "You'll be at the other end in about four minutes. Sit back and enjoy the ride. When you arrive, the hatch will automatically open. Get out, and close the hatch behind you. I'll send Tem and Jona on up."

Jon gave her a thumbs up and she closed the hatch. The tram slowly began accelerating toward its destination.

Jon lay back on the form-fitting seat, which was very comfortable, and had a momentary flashback of being back in the King's interview room. He sat up hurriedly, watching the tunnel lights go by faster and faster.

He called back to Kiala, "How you doing back there?" He looked back and saw that her eyes were firmly closed.

"I'm in an open field and it's sunny and the sky is blue, and we'll be there in three minutes and fourteen seconds."

"Hang in there," he said.

The tram arrived at the opposite control station. When the opened the hatch, emergency lights came on, bathing the room in a somber, red glow.

This control station was quite a bit larger than the one they had left.

When Tem and Jona arrived, Tem jumped out and said, "That was cool, can we do that again?"

Kiala said, "No."

A few minutes later, Anie got out of the tram, hurried to a side panel and turned on the primary power.

She activated a display and said, "I'm going to lock the maintenance tram here, in case anybody down at the other end wants to follow us."

Kiala asked, "How do you know so much about this?"

Anie blushed a little and said, "I had a boyfriend who worked for the Tram Authority. We spent a lot of time riding around. It was great fun," she said wistfully.

"We're here, now what?" asked Jona.

"We go see what we can see," said Jon.

They consulted a wallmap on the Concourse level.

Jon said, "Let's head for the Administrative levels. That'll be our best chance to find any computers or data storage units we can tap."

Jona said, "Agreed."

Kiala added, "The admin levels would probably also have sleeping quarters and kitchens."

"Yes, food. Excellent," said Tem. "I definitely think I can eat now."

"How is everybody holding up?" asked Jon.

Anie said, "I could go to sleep right now standing here."

"We'll look for a safe place after we've explored the admin level," Jon said.

Tem squinted at another wallmap and said, "There seem to be an awful lot of laboratories here for an administrative facility."

Jon said, "We'll have to ponder that later. Right now, let's find a secure place to spend the night."

Jona yawned. "That's an excellent idea. Make sure it has kitchen facilities. I'm getting hungry again."

"The map shows some temporary living quarters up one level from here. And, oh, this is a break, there's a computer facility right down this corridor," said Tem.

"OK, we'll take a quick look at the computer facilities, then head upstairs to get settled in for the night."

The computer facility was a suite of rooms, with a development lab, a supercooled test area, a data library, and an unfinished production area.

"Wow," Jona said as they walked through the area. "They had some really neat stuff to play with. Tem, help me scrounge some power sources and let's see if we can get these things to talk to us."

"It's too bad the station's not online, then we would have all the power we could ever hope to use," Kiala said, picking up a data crystal.

After Jona and Tem had managed to get a few of the larger computers running, she took her data tablet out of her pack and began trying to interface it with the main console.

Kiala found and brought up the inventory system.

Jon said, "It looks like you guys have enough to keep you busy. I'm going to go check out our accommodations for the night. Kiala and Anie, you have your PPDs ready?"

Jona was already deep into a search program. "That's fine. We'll be fine."

Jon said to Tem, "Come on, she won't come up for air for at least an hour."

He said to Kiala, "We won't be long. Keep your eyes and ears open."

"And don't shoot us," added Tem.

"Just hurry back," said Kiala.

The two men moved quietly up the stairs to the upper level. They found a plush suite of sleeping rooms joined by a central kitchen/work area. Each sleeping area could be sectioned off as a self-supporting apartment.

Tem whistled in admiration. "Very nice. Those geothermal guys knew how to live."

"Come on, let's see if there are any other ways in or out of this level."

As they methodically searched every room, Tem asked, "Do you think that the King's army could have followed us here?"

Jon answered, "Not likely, but possible. And we don't know who else is down here, remember. It wouldn't be reasonable to think that every inhabitant of the Labyrinth was somehow connected to the King."

"I suppose not," said Tem.

Satisfied that the area was secure, they went back to get Jona, Kiala, and Anie.

When they got back to the computer facility, they found all three women staring intently at a display.

"Hi kids, what you looking at?" Tem shouted.

Kiala jumped. "Don't ever do that again," she scolded.

Jona had not taken her eyes off the display.

Jon moved closer. "What is that? What did you find?"

Jona pointed to a section of the display. "I think it's our way out of here."

"When I was snooping around, I found the master map of the entire geothermal project. It shows every section of the project, completed or not, all the way down to the planet's core.

"But see this," she pointed to several lines, "what grabbed my attention were these things – power shafts that run directly to the surface from the core.

"And, there are several that lead to the surface on the opposite side of the planet. If we could figure out a way to get to one of the other power shafts, we could get out of here."

She pointed to another section of the map. "It looks like there is a tube network just above the core that connects all the power shafts. They can't be guarded, nobody's probably made it down this far before."

"I don't know about that, but go on", Jon said.

"So, we just take those elevators down until we get to the core tramline, take a tram to the other side...."

"Then Up and Out!" said Kiala.

"Do you have all this saved on crystal?" Jon asked.

"Working on it," said Jona. "How do our accommodations look?"

"Safe and comfy," said Tem.

"I don't know about anyone else, but I could use a shower, some food, and some sleep," said Jona.

"Me too," said Anie,

"Me three," said Kiala, and they all laughed.

They went back to the upper level kitchen and ate dinner in thoughtful silence.

After the meal, they brought beds in from the other suites so that they all slept in the same room. They had been together for so long that this protective arrangement now seemed natural.

Yawning, Tem asked, "What's the plan for tomorrow?"

Jon said, "See what else we can drag out of here and keep going."

"Down is Out," Tem said, and for the first time, it made sense.

Chapter 15

Jon slept uneasily that night. He didn't know if he was just too exhausted to rest properly, or they seemed to have a real chance of escaping, or they were so close to such an enormous source of power that had been abandoned so long ago.

At any rate, he drifted off in the early morning and woke to the sounds of breakfast. Everyone was already up, and gathered in the kitchen.

Jon shuffled over to the table and sat down. Anie handed him a steaming cup of coffee.

"Thanks Anie," he said.

Taking a sip of her tea, Jona asked, "OK, what now?"

Jon said, "Did you get all the information you could out of the station's memory?"

Jona said, "No, there's a lot more."

"OK, then why don't you take Tem and Kiala and go back and see what you can find. Anie and I will scavenge for equipment."

"What do you think is in the other computers?" asked Tem, who helped himself to another waffle.

"Dunno," replied Jona. The subsystems I couldn't get into were too tightly encrypted, so it's logical to assume that they contain some pretty important stuff."

"Like payroll records," offered Kiala.

Jona said, "Could be. I hope we find more that that, though. When I was going through the security schematics for this place, I saw one big hurdle: the elevators."

Jon swallowed a bite of eggs. "What about the elevators?" he asked.

"I'll keep looking, of course, "Jona explained, "but the ones that lead down to the next level of the station are locked, with really really tight encryption – for all practical purposes unbreakable, unless you have a few hundred quantum computers and several months to wait."

Jon said, "Hmmm."

Jona paused. "Actually, that's not all. I don't know if this was intentional or not, but the elevator entrance is blocked by several tons of rubble. There may have been a cave in, or it might have been sabotage."

"But I thought that somebody's plan was to put the project on hold, not kill it."

Jon finished his coffee and said, "Not everybody plays on the same team."

He stood up and said, "Let's be on our toes today – who knows, if Jona's right about the sabotage, there may be more traps around here. Be careful."

The group left for their respective tasks in a distinctly less enthusiastic mood.

Jon and Anie began their search for additional equipment in one of several warehouses on the perimeter of the building. Walking through the first warehouse, they both marveled at how much stuff there was, and that it had all been left behind. They passed garages containing heavy-duty haulers and transports, and smaller, faster transport vehicles.

Kicking the tires of one of the transports as she passed, Anie said, "We could have really used this thing back there."

Jon checked the cargo area of the transport and said, "Yep, it's a shame we can't use it now."

Anie said, "Why not?"

Jon looked up at her. "I assumed that the elevators were too small to carry vehicles."

Anie shook her head. "No, the elevators are big. Jona showed the schematics to me. It's worth a try."

"You're right about that," Jon said.

"Can't that thing over there be attached to the transport?" She pointed to an earthmoving attachment leaning against the wall.

"Yes, it can," said Jon.

"Wouldn't that be helpful in clearing out rubble, say, rubble that was blocking a certain elevator?"

Jon brightened. "I believe it would be."

———

Back in the computer facility, Jona, Tem, and Kiala all worked on unlocking and restarting as many systems as they could. Jona had gotten lucky and found a hardcopy of disaster recovery procedures that contained access keys, encryption algorithms, and passwords.

Tem skimmed the summary nodes of one of the unlocked servers and looked up in confusion.

"This is odd. Hey, you guys, why would a geothermal research system need a complete map of the human genome?"

"What?" asked Jona and came over to look over Tem's shoulder.

"That is strange. Maybe it's a computer they got from somewhere else and hadn't had a chance to reallocate the data."

"I don't think so," said Kiala. "Look, the log entries show that this data was accessed by other systems in this building."

"OK, fine," said Jona, going back to her own research.

Several minutes later, she looked up. "I just found a reference to a computer with ID MAT-5927 that may have something to do with controlling the elevator system. Start looking for it, OK?"

"Right," said Tem. "I'll go look in the Production area – I think I saw some MAT-level systems in there."

Jona walked over beside Kiala and sat down at the display Tem had just been looking at.

"Now, let's see what this genome mystery is about."

Frowning, she placed several icons beside each other and then opened a command window, where she typed a sequence of letters and numbers so long that Kiala couldn't begin to guess what she was trying to do.

She entered the command and waited as the computer processed her instructions. After a few seconds, an icon blinked, and Jona ran her fingers through her hair. "Tem was right. This is exceedingly odd."

She pointed to one of the icons. "This system was some sort of repository for genetic research. But," she touched the blinking icon, "all the data associated with the research was deleted. All of it. The only things that are left are the support and reference information."

Kiala asked, "What does it mean?"

Jona said, "Like I should know? Let's go see if Tem has found that computer yet."

———————

Jon and Anie had managed to start the transport, and working together, they had even gotten the earthmoving attachment hooked up. They drove slowly to the next warehouse.

Jon scanned the labels beside each cargo area.

"What are we looking for?" asked Anie.

"Heatsuits, to protect us as we get closer to the planetary core. I see some in those lockers over there."

They stopped and examined several of the suits.

Designed for geothermal exploration and research, heatsuits were capable of absorbing and redirecting massive amounts of heat.

Jon said, "Let's get several suits, at least two for everybody and as many power cells as we can find. We don't want to run out of power cells when we're wearing these things."

Jon pulled down one of the suits. "Do you think this will fit Kiala?"

She laughed and said, "Um, no. You'd better let me pick out the sizes. And I won't tell Kiala that you think she's fifty pounds heavier than she really is."

Jon stammered, "I didn't, I didn't mean to..."

She giggled. "I said I won't tell."

They gathered several suits for each of the group, and three suits that could be worn by any of them in an emergency.

Anie asked, "Are the power cells still good? I mean, they've been down here a while. Don't they eventually lose their charge?"

"That's a good question. There should be a charger around here somewhere."

Anie went into a closet and came back with a metal rack with enclosures for five power cells. "Is this it?" she asked.

"There it is. You know, you're getting pretty good at this."

"Thanks, I like to shop for new clothes."

They put the heatsuits and the powercells and charger in the cargo area of the transport.

"OK, what next?" asked Anie.

Jon said, "Well, I don't know about you, but if we could find some clothes other than the ones we have on, I'd feel better."

"Ooh, me too. There must be some kind of central laundry around here somewhere."

"Imagine, we might even find some coveralls with pockets."

"Ahh, pockets, now there was an invention."

They located a laundry, and selected clean, if not exactly fresh, coveralls for everyone. Anie also found a store of boots, coats, and socks.

Jon said, "I don't know if we'll need the coats."

Anie said, "We don't know what the weather will be like on the other side, do we? We might come up in one of the polar regions."

"I hadn't thought of that. OK, put them on the pile."

Surveying the stack of items they had gathered, Jon said, "It's a good thing we have this transport. I'd hate to have to carry all this stuff."

———

Tem had located the computer Jona was looking for, and now Jona was studiously trying to get the computer to start. She had tried several times, but each time, the computer asked for a password, and the password in her documentation didn't work.

She sat in front of its display, considering her options.

Kiala said, "If you can't access it directly, why not try to get one of the systems in the other room ask it for something. You might not know the password, but maybe one of the other systems does?"

Annoyed, Jona tried to sound casual. "Yeah, I was going to do that next. Tem, found any other computers with strange filesystems?" she asked, still not trying Kiala's solution.

Tem said, "No, that one gave me the creeps. Plus, there are quite a few labs around here that aren't indicated in the building summaries."

Judging that enough time had passed, Jona went into the development lab to another computer, found the reference to MAT-5927, and made a data request from that system.

Just as Kiala had predicted, the two systems connected immediately, and Jona was in. After a few minutes of tweaking, the filesystem of MAT-5927 lay open in front of her.

"Did it work?" asked Kiala, coming from the other room.

"Yup, no problems," said Jona airily.

Kiala said, "That was a good idea, wasn't it?"

Jona said, "Fine. Yes it was, now will you stop gloating?"

"OK," Kiala said, and went back into the Production area, a big smile on her face.

After a few minutes, Jona found what she was looking for – an encryption catalog for the elevator security systems.

Using this information, and the new hyperfast computer they had discovered in the other room, they should be able to generate the unlock codes for the elevators all the way down and back up the other side.

———————

Jon and Anie found several other useful items on their scavenger hunt – including first aid kits. On the way back, Anie asked to drive the transport, and Jon was again impressed by her skill and resourcefulness.

They parked the transport in a storage bay and walked up to the sleeping area to meet the others for lunch.

"How was your morning?" Jon asked.

"Lots of new stuff to digest, but I'm confident I can unlock the elevators now."

"Excellent, because we, or rather Anie, found something that will help us move all that debris away from the elevator."

"Really?" asked Tem.

Still feeling pleased with herself, Anie said, "Yup."

Taking a tray from the heating unit, Tem said, "Cool beans."

Jona asked, "What did you find?"

"One of those multi-purpose transports with the attachment thing on the front."

"Good, I'm tired of walking all the time."

Jon asked Jona, "What did you find? Anything interesting?"

Jona shrugged. "Some odd stuff."

"Odd? In what way?"

Mark W. Burris

"Odd meaning that the data was in no way, shape, or form related to geothermal anything."

"What was it related to?"

"Genetics."

"Genetics?"

Jona said, "Yeah, and this is the weird thing – all the data on the computer, except for reference material, had been deleted."

"Maybe it was somebody's personal project..." Jon said doubtfully.

"Down here? I don't think so." said Jona. "Besides, other systems in this building were accessing the data."

"OK," said Jon. "Is it worth investigating?"

Jona said, "It would take time to reconstruct the erased data. We could do it..."

"We don't have the time. Let's concentrate on getting the elevator working."

"Agreed."

After a quick rest, Jon, Tem, and Anie drove the transport to the elevator entrance and began moving the massive pile of rubble away from the elevator.

By dinnertime, they all were tired, sweaty, and dusty. They had cleared most of the rubble away from the entrance, but there was still work to do to make a clear path for the transport.

Wiping his forehead with a dirty sleeve, Jon said, "Let's call it a day and head back. I could use a hot shower."

"Me too," said Anie. "We should start charging those heatsuit power cells. How long do they take to charge? We've got a bunch."

Jon said, "About two hours per cell. We'll have to find a working substation we can hook into tomorrow. Oh, my back is hurting."

Tem groaned in sympathy. "I'm not used to this either. I'm a knowledge worker!"

Anie tut-tutted, "Oh, you poor things. We'd better run back and get you into the shower before you complain to death."

Jon laughed and said, "I'm not sure, but I think we've been insulted."

Tem said, "I'm sure."

They went back to the sleeping area and got ready for dinner. Despite the occasional groans from overworked muscles, the group's mood was distinctly better. One more day of effort and they would be ready to unlock the elevator.

After dinner, Jon asked Jona and Kiala to get them all up to speed about their digital foraging that day.

Jona said, "I've downloaded anything useful I could think of into your tablets – maps....oh, I forgot, I found these in a locker near the computer facility."

She took several wristbands from her pack and handed them out.

Anie asked, "What are they?"

"Short-range communicators. I thought that since we were spending more time apart, those might come in handy," Jona said.

Jon examined his wristband. "This model also has a locator system. Have you tried it out?"

Jona looked at her wristband. "No, I didn't know it could do that. But it can't get a fix on a satellite this far underground, can it?"

"No, but I'm hoping that we can use them to find each other if one of us gets lost. The tracking system should be able to indicate distance and direction."

"What about the range?" Tem asked.

Jon said, "Should be about the same as the range of the communicator – maybe twenty miles best case. Down here, though, if there's a lot of metal ore in the surrounding rocks, a mile or less."

"Still," he said, "these will come in handy. Jona, did you find a tagging or calibration program to go with these?"

"I'm still reading the documentation, but I should be able to get everybody set up tomorrow morning."

"Tagging?" asked Kiala in a concerned voice. Visions of painful procedures came to her. "That sounds like it would hurt."

Jon smiled and said, "It's nothing like that. You put the device on, and the tagging program reads your unique electromagnetic signature. That, and the unique id of the device itself serves to identify you to the tracking program."

"Oh. That's good, I think," she said doubtfully.

"Any more ideas about, what was it, that genetic data on that computer?"

Tem shook his head. "No. Maybe multiple research projects going on at once down here? I don't know. Goodness knows why you would do biology this far underground."

"Unless the research had a direct bearing on the geothermal project," said Kiala. "Maybe somebody was studying the long-term effect of core radiation on humans, or the psychological stress of living so far underground."

Jona said, "Yeah. That sounds plausible."

"Sounds good to me," Tem said.

Jon stretched and winced as his back muscles reminded him of the morning's activity. "Ow, that sounds great. I'm going to get some sleep. We'll saddle up early tomorrow, get the remaining rubble moved, and take our shot at the elevator."

Jon had planned to keep watch at least several hours, but woke with a start sometime after midnight. Still sore from the previous day, he wandered into the kitchen in search of some aspirin. The room was illuminated only by the ghostly glow of the security monitors Jona had set up.

He watched the monitors for several minutes, having a strange feeling that somebody was watching them. He took one last look at the displays and went back to bed.

<hr />

The next morning everyone was eager to get back to the elevator area and finish the cleanup job. Anie and Kiala went to get the transport while Jon and Tem cleared a path to one of the access panels for Jona.

She climbed over the remaining rubble, and examined the panel.

"Did we bring those prying bars?"

Tem said, "Yep, right here." He started to place the end of one of the bars against the panel.

"Hold on. May I?" asked Jona.

"Oh." said Tem, "Be my guest."

Taking the bar, Jona said, "It's not like I don't appreciate the help, but there are some delicate optical crystals in there. If they've survived this long, I'd hate to break them now. A little room please?"

Tem backed away as Jona deftly inserted an end of the bar into a barely visible slot in the side of the panel. With a flick of the bar, she had the panel open.

Tem whispered to Jon, "I keep forgetting she's a pro."

Jon nodded and asked, "What's the verdict?"

Jona crawled part of the way inside the maintenance area. She said in a muffled voice, "Better than I expected." She crawled back out, coughing from the dust, and continued, "Some of the crystals are cracked, but I thought they would be, so I found some spares yesterday."

She unrolled a protective sheet of multicolored crystals.

"These should be all we need."

They looked down the corridor to see Anie and Kiala coming toward them in the transport. Kiala was driving, and Anie had her feet stuck out the side window.

Kiala stopped the transport, and jumped down. "I wish we had found this a lot earlier."

Jon said, "Better late than never. Anie, are you ready?"

Anie scooted over into the driver's seat, and skillfully moved a large boulder out of the way.

Jona said, "I'd swear she's done this before."

"At this rate, we'll be finished in no time," said Tem.

They watched as she deftly maneuvered among the rubble.

As Tem predicted, in under half an hour Anie cleared a sufficient area in front of both the access panel and the elevator entrance so Jona could work completely unobstructed.

Jon asked Jona, "How long before we can try to open the door?"

She stuck her head out of the hatch and said, "Give me about 20 minutes. Tem, hand me that welder."

Tem reached into a pack and brought out a portable power welder. "Here you go."

"Thanks," she said, and disappeared into the hatch.

"In the meantime, I'll get some more power cells from the warehouse. Moving all those big rocks pretty much drained the ones on board," said Anie.

"Good idea," said Jon. "If all goes well, we'll be on our way."

"I'll go with you," said Tem.

Jon went over to the hatch, where only Jona's feet were visible.

"How's it going?" he asked.

"Shut up and leave me alone. I'm almost finished."

Jon smiled. He had a good feeling about today.

Just them, he heard the squealing of tires and looked down the corridor to see the transport heading toward them, moving very fast.

At first he thought the transport wasn't going to stop, and he grabbed Jona's feet to get her out of harm's way.

"What the, what are you doing?" she spluttered.

The transport screeched to a stop right in front of the door, and Anie and Tem jumped out of the vehicle.

"We've got company," they said breathlessly.

Chapter 16

They activated one of Jona's monitors and watched as several dozen men entered the warehouse area.

"The King's men?" asked Tem.

"Who else could it be?"

Jona ducked back in the maintenance hatch.

Jon thought furiously. They could stay here and hide (or fight), they could slip out, and try to hide in the rest of the Labyrinth. Or they could go down the elevator. *If* Jona could get them in. And *if* it was still running. And *if* they could do all that before the King's men found them.

Jon said, "Jona?"

Jona crawled out of the maintenance hatch, closed and sealed the door.

"Shut up," she explained.

Everyone waited tensely, watching the King's men move closer and closer.

Finally Jona said, "OK. Keep your fingers crossed. Here goes."

She touched an icon on her tablet and waited. Nothing happened.

"Jona?" asked Jon, a definite edge in his voice.

"OK, give me a minute. I didn't expect to pop it on the first try."

The King's men moved closer.

Tem said, "Jon, we might need a Plan B."

"I was just thinking that."

He pointed down the corridor in the opposite direction to the warehouse. "Where does that go?"

"There's another loading dock down there. Come to think of it..." he began.

"We could get squeezed from both ends of the corridor."

"Jona?"

"Leave me alone!"

She frantically moved icons around on her tablet.

"OK, I think I've got it. Go." The elevator door didn't move.

Jon said, "Everybody in the transport. Now."

Jona said, "Wait, wait, I can do this."

He grabbed her and pulled her toward the vehicle. "Then do it in the truck."

They all bundled in the truck, with Jon in the driver's seat and Jona hunched over in the back, feverishly jabbing at her tablet.

She said, "OK, I've got it."

The elevator door made an enormous grinding noise, as it slowly began to open.

"Yes!" shouted Jona.

Anie said, "They can see us now."

Dozens of armed men appeared at the end of the corridor.

"Jona, will the elevator work?"

"Do I look like an elevator inspector?"

Jon considered their options: assume the elevator would not work, and run down the opposite corridor, and hope that the King's men had not surrounded the building; or go for it. He made his choice in an instant.

"Let's go for it."

But when he pressed the forward accelerator, nothing happened. The power meters all registered zero.

"Tem, did you change the cells?"

Tem looked at the display. "Yes. All of them."

No one moved.

"Wait. Hold on," Tem said, and jumped out of the transport. By now the men were close enough to fire at the transport. With PPD bursts scattering around him, Tem flung open the power access and reattached the cable from the cell to the vehicle. The power meters jumped to one hundred percent.

They were now less than fifty feet away.

"Get in!" yelled Jon, and as Tem fell in to the back seat, Jon moved the vehicle into the elevator.

Jona said, "Going down?" and pressed several icons in rapid succession. The great doors closed and the elevator began moving downward.

Sitting back in his seat, Jon wiped his forehead. "That was too close."

Kiala said, "You can say that again."

Tem said, "Jona, you are the greatest!"

Jona said, "Now give me a little time and keep out of my face. I'm going to scramble the lock code before the termites up there have a chance to get in and do some damage."

"Can they do that?" Kiala asked.

"Possibly. But after I replaced the crystals, I welded the access panel shut. Unless they have a cutting torch handy, they won't be able to get in until we're down on the lower level."

"What happens if they just smash the controls?" asked Tem.

"The elevator follows its current instructions," said Jona.

Tem asked, "How long before we get to the next level?"

Jona consulted her schematic of the geothermal station.

"About four hours."

Kiala sat back, "So now what do we do?"

Jon said, "Enjoy the ride."

Tem asked, "Are we there yet?"

"That's not funny."

Tem said, "I'm going to get out and walk around."

Jona said, "Walk around in circles?"

"We've got four hours."

"OK, I'll go too."

They climbed down from the vehicle, and Tem walked around to the rear, and said, "Oh, boy."

Jona followed him. "What is it?"

"Look at this."

An impact blast had dented the shielding right beside the access to the power cells. "If that had been a foot to the right, we wouldn't have made it."

"Thank goodness for small favors. I think I'll get back in the vehicle."

For the next few hours, they slept, talked, and played games on the display tablets. After a while, the hum of the elevator became hypnotic, then faded to background noise.

Finally, they were minutes away from reaching the lower level. The elevator's hum deepened as it slowed down before arrival.

"Jona, are the tablets able to access any of the security cameras on this level?" Jon asked.

"Yup, looks like we can see the elevator entrance and several corridors, more warehouses, sleeping quarters.... The schematic is similar to the level above, except there are fewer administrative and research areas. We're getting down to the nitty-gritty."

"Any sign of....movement?" Tem asked.

"Can't see any, but it's pretty dark down there."

"Infrared?"

"I'm not very good at looking at these things. Jon, you wanna take a look?"

She handed Jon the tablet, and he studied the camera output for several minutes, switching from one view to another, zooming closer on several objects.

"I don't see any heat signatures – at least any that would indicate people or animals."

The elevator came to a stop. "Well, we're here," said Jona. "Opening the door."

She touched an icon, and the door opened slowly. They peered into the gloom ahead. Jon switched on the headlights and slowly drove into the corridor.

"Wait," said Jona. "Before we go any farther." She jumped out of the vehicle, opened the access panel, and took out several of the crystals. She put the crystals into her pocket, and climbed back into the transport.

"Now, even if they can break into the panel up top, they can't make the elevator go back up unless they know a whole bunch more about this system than I think they do."

They slowly drove through the wide corridors, passing bays full of construction equipment.

"Let's find the sleeping area and kitchen," suggested Kiala.

Looking at his copy of the level schematics, Jon said, "We're heading there now."

They stopped at the end of the corridor and parked the transport in an unused bay.

"We'll lock the vehicle in here," said Jon.

They took their packs from the cargo section, and walked through several smaller maintenance bays before arriving at a dorm area.

This dorm was larger, but less elegant, than their previous accommodations.

Jon surveyed several sleeping quarters, and chose a smaller area, adjacent to the infirmary and kitchen.

In the kitchen they found several lockers with more than adequate supplies of food and water.

They found sheets, pillows, and blankets in a hallway closet. Tem and Anie located a power panel, and managed to tap into the infirmary's independent batteries to provide them with light and power.

Jon and Tem again walked the perimeter of the area. They found nothing to indicate that anyone, or anything, had been on this level for years. Despite the relatively clean appearance of the level, it had a cold, abandoned feel to it.

Jon was glad to return to the light and warmth of the dorm and kitchen.

"What's for supper?"

Kiala walked with him over to the locker. "Help yourself."

"What looks good?" he asked.

She selected a pasta dish with vegetables. "This is what I'm having."

As they sat in the kitchen eating their meals, Anie asked, "I wonder whatever happened to Deemus?"

Jona made a face. "Why? I don't."

"Well, he was pretty much right about all this, now wasn't he?"

Until that moment, Jon had forgotten about what Deemus had said about the Labyrinth. Anie was right, except for the omission of the King of the Labyrinth, his information had been surprisingly accurate.

"I wonder how he knew so much about the Labyrinth if no one ever returned?" asked Tem.

"Good question," said Jona. "I think maybe Deemus was more than he let on."

"You think the crazy thing was just an act?" asked Jon, slurping his soup.

"I don't know. Now that I have a chance to think about it, I just felt...manipulated."

"I think that was the prison doing its job."

"You know, all that seems so long ago," said Kiala.

"Another lifetime," added Tem.

"Another lifetime," repeated Jon, and immediately thought of Lara. They had been moving so fast for the past several days, he had not thought of her once. He bit his lip.

Noticing his reaction, Kiala asked, "Are you OK?"

He cleared his throat and answered, "Yeah, I'm fine."

Jona said, "You were thinking about Lara."

"Yeah."

"From what you said about her in your interrogation, she's a strong lady, she'll be OK."

He looked at Jona for several seconds. "I hope you're right. Let's get some sleep."

After the others had all crawled under the covers in their cots, Jon lay awake, staring at the ceiling.

They had been lucky so far. He hoped their luck would last.

He tossed and turned for the next hour, listening to the regular breathing of the others. As she had done at their earlier sanctuary, Jona had hooked up several display tablets to the building's security cameras. From his cot, Jon could just see the images, which cast a ghostly light over the room.

After an hour, Jon decided not to fight sleep any longer and got up to make himself a cup of tea. He padded silently to the kitchen, found a clean cup, and looked in the locker for some tea bags. Behind some freeze-dried coffee, he found some jasmine tea in foil pouches. He poured some water in the cup and put it in the microwave. While the water was heating, he opened a foil pouch and inhaled the rich scent of jasmine.

He let the tea steep in the hot water for several minutes, savoring the fragrant steam. He closed his eyes and tried to get his brain to slow down.

He took a sip of the tea, and tried to concentrate on the hotness of the liquid, the taste of the jasmine flowers, the warmth of the cup in his hands, the heat falling down his throat, his breathing, in and out, deep and slow...

Faith, that's what he needed. Faith in his Creator, that He was in control; faith that Lara was all right, faith that he and his companions would persevere, faith that when they did escape, they could expose this corrupt system and restart this facility, which could provide energy to fuel a new economic renaissance for his planet...

He took another sip, and tried to clear him mind. Before long, he found himself relaxing. Eventually he yawned, finished his tea, and went back to bed. He closed his eyes and slept. He did not dream.

Chapter 17

The next day saw the group once more in exploration mode. They quickly located the second elevator that would take them further downward. Unlike the first elevator, this one was completely intact, and Jona unlocked the elevator door on the first try.

Beyond the elevator corridor were several labs containing more computers and data storage modules.

Wearing their communicators, the group split up, with Kiala and Anie going off to explore beyond the original elevator. Tem, Jon, and Jona peered into the darkened computer area.

"Let's see what we can find in here," Jona said.

"I don't know," Jon replied. "We have complete schematics of the plant, don't we?"

"Well, yeah, but there could be more useful information here."

"Tem?"

"Might as well. It's not like anybody else is going to care."

"You're beginning to sound like Jona," Jon said.

Tem laughed, "Don't worry. I'm not contemplating a career change. I just want to get out of here."

Tem went to locate the lighting panel for the computer labs. By the time he returned, Jon and Jona had the door open.

"We got lights; we got power, what kind of data do we got?" Tem asked.

Jona rapidly scanned one of the catalog servers.

"It looks like these were mostly specialized automation servers – the ones that controlled and maintained the automated equipment on these levels – I don't see any research or security data. Pretty much the nuts and bolts of geothermal station maintenance, I'd imagine."

Disappointed, Tem asked, "Any mention of genomes or biological studies?"

Jona looked again. "Nope, nothing."

They searched through the remaining computers in the lab, but found nothing else interesting or useful.

They were about to go through another room when Jon's communicator beeped. The sound surprised him, and it took him a second or two to respond.

"Jon, are you there?" It was Kiala and she sounded worried.

"Yeah, sorry, go ahead."

"Is Jona there?"

Jona spoke into her own communicator. "I'm here. What's up?"

"Um, we were walking past the elevator car we came down on last night..."

"And," prompted Jon.

"And it seems to have gone back up the shaft."

Jona said, "What? But I locked it. It couldn't have returned by itself unless..."

"Unless someone called it back up," Jon said.

"I didn't think that bunch had it in them. I guess I was wrong."

Jon thought a minute. "Jona, can you tell when the elevator was summoned?"

She consulted her tablet. "I think the system keeps log records."

"Try to find out when it left. I want to know how much time we have before we can expect visitors."

She frowned in concentration, fingers hovering just over the tablet, moving icons with practiced skill.

Finally she said, "I can do better than tell you when it left. I can tell you when it arrived on the upper level, and when it started back down."

"It's already on its way down?" Tem asked in alarm.

"Yup, two hours away."

"Then don't we need to be making our way to the down elevator?" asked Kiala.

"Hey, guys, it's all right. I just stopped the elevator. I think if you give me a few more minutes, I can get it to go back up."

But just as she opened up another workspace on her tablet, she sputtered.

Jon said, "What?"

Clearly flustered, Jona said, "Apparently, they're moving downward again. They broke my lock. Let me try again." Her fingers flew over the tablet.

"There. Let's see them break *that*."

"What's happening?" asked Anie.

"Nothing to worry about...huh?" She checked her display.

She said, "They're moving downward again!"

She did a double-take on her display. "And, they've found a way to make the elevator descend faster."

"What's their estimated time of arrival?" asked Jon.

After a few seconds of calculation, Jona said, "Forty-three minutes."

"OK," said Jon. "We're leaving."

———————

They met back at the sleeping area, gathered and refilled their packs, and hurried down to the transport.

As they opened the doors, Tem said, "We've got an idea."

"All right," said Jon. "Let's hear it."

Jona said, "How about welding the door shut?"

"They'll just cut through it," countered Jon.

"*If* they have the equipment, and even then it will cost them time."

"How quickly can you do it?" asked Jon.

"Ten minutes, tops. Worst case, it'll take them at least that long to cut it."

"OK, do it."

"Anie said, "How about blocking the door with heavy stuff? There's plenty around here to use."

She swept her hand around the bay, which held heavy mining equipment.

"Hey, that's not a bad idea, either."

"There's an earth mover in the next bay. I saw it when we were exploring this morning," she said.

"OK, get to work. But remember," he called to them as they headed toward the elevator. "We leave in fifteen minutes. No later."

Jona, with Tem's help, welded the door shut in record time. Anie used the earthmover to drag several pieces of heavy mining equipment out of the bay.

"Will you guys hurry up?" Anie complained.

"OK, ok, give us a minute," Jona said impatiently.

She and Tem cleared out, and Anie pushed several tons of metal against the elevator door.

"That should stop them for a while," she said, jumping down from the earthmover. Before she left, she opened a hatch on the side of the earthmover and took out the starter and put it in her pocket.

Jon drove up in a hurry.

"Ok, guys, fourteen minutes and counting, everybody get in. Time to leave."

The second elevator entrance was just across the corridor – less than a hundred feet. Jon gunned the engines, and the transport covered the distance in a few seconds.

Slowing down in front of the closed door, Jon said, "OK, Jona, do your magic."

Jona had already preprogrammed the sequence into her tablet. She casually flicked one icon, and the second elevator door began to open. Jon swung the transport around, and expertly backed in to the elevator car.

"OK, Down is Out."

Jona flicked another icon, the doors closed and the elevator began its descent.

This elevator was constructed differently from the first one. Although just as solidly built, the walls of this elevator were made of a strong polymer – incredibly strong, clear plastic. For the first hour or so, the shaft outside was dull rock, striated with mineral deposits here and there. But after an hour or so into the trip, Kiala looked outside the transport and gasped.

"Look!"

They had entered an enormous cavern with walls shot through with the most spectacular glowing minerals – green, fiery red, blue, gold, silver....

The photoluminescent rocks cast off enough light to illuminate the entire cavern.

Tem whistled, "Boy, those must be worth a fortune."

"No kidding," said Jona.

"They're beautiful," said Anie.

"It almost makes the trip worthwhile," said Kiala in wonder.

Jona scowled. "Only if we get to keep some of those rocks," she said.

They descended through several caverns like the first, some with fabulous riches of sparkling diamonds, veins of gold and luminescent minerals.

At one point, Anie said, "Is it just me, or is it getting hotter in here?"

Jon said, "I noticed that too. We can run the cooling system just a bit, but I want to save our batteries for when we really need them."

"Oh, not to worry, I'll just fan myself," Anie said.

They continued to descend, passing thorough caverns holding fortunes locked up in the earth.

Kiala asked, "How long before we get to the next level?"

Jona looked at her tablet. "Another thirty minutes or so."

Jon asked, "Can you see anything down there?"

"Not yet. It looks like this level was left unfinished. I don't know if it was built just to connect the elevators or what, but all I see down there is dark."

"Is it possible the camera system's batteries are tapped out."

"This close to a virtually limitless power supply? I'd have to say not. We'll just have to see what we can see when we get there."

As Jona predicted, about thirty minutes later, the elevator car eased to a stop, and she opened the doors.

The air that entered the car was hot and swirling with choking dust.

Coughing, Jon sealed the transport windows and said, "Put rebreathers on the scavenge list."

"Ugh. This is not going to be fun."

"We can spend the night in here if we have to."

Jon turned the headlights on.

"OK. Let's go see what we can see."

The transport's headlights made two bright rods in the darkness as they slowly drove down the dusty corridor.

Jona pointed to a structure that resembled an airlock up ahead. "What's that?" she asked.

"It looks like the best place to get out of this dust."

Jon eased the transport up to the side of the airlock and Tem jumped out into the storm, ran around the transport and secured the lock against the side of the transport.

Coughing and almost blinded, Tem fell back into the cabin.

"I hope whatever's on the other side of this has clean air, or at least something to help us deal with that mess outside." He slapped his pants, raising a small cloud of dust.

Jon stopped the engine and said, "Let's go see if we're in any better shape."

He led the way into the airlock. The door on the other side was locked, but Jona had it opened before Anie got out of the transport.

They entered the darkened room carefully. Jon found the room lights and turned them on, illuminating a control center of some sort. Jona found what she guessed was the main computer on this level and got it started.

Anie and Kiala started looking for masks, goggles, rebreathers, anything to help them combat the dust.

"Where are we?" asked Tem.

"According to these notes," said Jona, pointing to the computer display, "this level was unfinished. The dust storms are caused by the convection of air heated by the geothermal processes underneath."

"Where does the dust come from?" asked Tem.

"The notes indicate that the force of the air coming up from below scours the rocks on the way up, chipping off tiny particles."

"Sort of like natural sandblasting," mused Jon.

"Yeah."

"Well," said Kiala, it looks like we can hole up here for awhile. There are sleeping and eating areas in the rooms on the other side of this wall.

"We also found some airmasks and goggles. No need to walk around choking and squinting in this stuff."

"This 'weather' must be hard on the equipment," said Anie.

"I'll bet," said Jon.

Tem studied one of the consoles by the airlock. "This looks like it controls some sort of ventilation system in the tunnels. Maybe the builders figured out how to section off the tunnels from the storms and ventilate them."

"That would certainly save wear and tear on the machines down here."

"Not to mention the people."

"Right."

"It looks like we still have power. Let's see what happens. I'm going to try to close off and ventilate the area right outside."

He moved several icons toward a map of the level, and then entered a command. Outside, they heard a giant swoosh and saw some kind of force-field come shimmering into existence just beyond the elevator. They could then hear the sound of giant fans.

"Come on, let's go outside," said Tem.

"Wait!" said Kiala, "Put on your masks and goggles."

"Won't need them," said Tem. "But we'll take them as insurance."

They walked out the airlock and found that all the dust had been blown away. The fans produced a stiff but not unpleasant breeze.

It was fascinating to stand right beside the force-field, close enough to feel the tingle of the enormous energies used, and see the blizzard-like conditions on the other side.

They walked back to the control room and went through the customary ritual of securing the area, evaluating the contents of the food lockers, setting up the display tablets, and picking the cots they would sleep on that night.

After a decent hot meal of rehydrated stew, everyone was ready to settle down for the night. For some reason – maybe it was the severity of the storm safely contained outside and the force-fields protecting them – Jon felt safer here than anywhere else he had been underground. This night, he had absolutely no trouble falling asleep.

He dreamed that he was rising slowly upward in the elevator shaft, passing the fantastic mineral-rich caverns, glowing with unimaginable wealth. He felt slightly cold and heavy, but buoyant, as if he were under water. It was a very pleasant feeling, floating upward. He stretched out his arms and legs and closed his eyes.

When he opened them, he was no longer in the elevator shaft, but floating upward in the middle of a cavern. He found that by altering the position of his arms and legs, he could move sideways. He swooped upward toward a wall striated with alternating bands of vibrant blue and red minerals. As he stretched his hand out toward the wall, he felt a soft heat. He reached out and felt the wall, and to his surprise, it was soft to the touch. He stroked the warm softness of the wall as he drifted up. He looked upward and saw that the ceiling of the cavern had opened up onto a brilliant blue sky, flecked with white puffy clouds. He could feel a warm breeze enter the cavern, and felt himself slowing down. The light from above got more intense, and the breeze turned into a hot wind, pushing him downward.

Suddenly he became sickeningly aware that he was falling. He reached out toward the glowing wall, trying to find a handhold, something to grab onto. He fell faster and faster. Downwards to the molten core below. And as he fell, he could feel the heat on his skin, at first uncomfortable, then growing in intensity. Soon he was in an agony of pain.

But as he got closer and closer to the core, he began to fall more slowly, and soon he was being carried up again by the hot painful winds coming from the heated air rising up from the angry core. As he rose, he again could move at will, and he floated toward another wall, this one sparkling with thousands of diamonds and veins of gold. He reached out to touch the gold, and it was again, warm and soft to the touch. But then he felt the gold move beneath his hand...

───────

He awoke with a start, the memory of the softness still fresh in his mind. In fact, the dream was so real, he imagined that his arm still tingled from the contact with the rock. He lay still in the cot, listening.

The room was dark and quiet, illuminated only by Jona's ever-present security monitors. He could hear only the regular breathing of his fellows. Then he felt a pressure on his arm. It was unmistakable – a soft, furry hand was touching his arm.

He lunged out to grab whatever it was, but, before he could, the dark figure scurried away. He yelled, threw his covers back, and jumped out of his cot, racing toward the door.

Startled awake, the others groped for lights.

"What happened?" asked Jona.

"Where's Jon?"

"I saw him running out the door," said Tem.

"Look at the monitors," said Jona, and they all crowded around the displays.

"What's he's chasing?" asked Anie.

They looked in fascination as Jon chased the intruder through corridors and warehouses. It was too dark to get a good image of the intruder, and infrared only revealed that it was a small creature that ran on two legs.

Jon stumbled and fell several times in the darkness. Each time, the intruder gained distance on him until Jon found himself alone and winded in one of the larger warehouses.

Jon came limping back, holding his arm.

"Did you get a good look at whoever it was?" he asked.

"Sort of. Actually no, it was too dark," Jona said.

"Tell me about it," Jon replied, rubbing his arm.

"It looked like a monkey," said Anie.

"Yeah," said Tem.

"But what would a monkey be doing down here?" asked Jon.

"And how could a monkey elude Jona's alarm system?" asked Tem.

"I don't know," said Jona, "the alarms should have been able to detect anything as small as a rat."

Kiala made a face. "Don't talk about rats. I feel like a rat in a maze already."

Jona checked the alarm systems, and raised her eyebrows several times before she finally said, "Well, that explains why the alarms didn't go off."

"Why?"

"Somebody turned them off."

"The monkey?" asked Kiala in astonishment. "That's impossible."

"Apparently not," said Jon.

"I don't know if I can get back to sleep now," said Kiala.

"Me either," said Anie.

Jon said, "It's almost morning anyway, and I'm going to try to find out where that monkey went."

They got dressed, ate a hurried breakfast, and gathered at the entrance to the warehouse. Tem channeled some power into the area and turned on the lights.

"Let's split up. I'll retrace my footsteps – except for the falls – in this warehouse. Jona and Tem, you cover the lower warehouse down the corridor. Kiala and Anie, you cover the upper warehouse. There are no other possible exit points in this direction on this level. Right, Jona?"

"No possible exit points for people; I don't know about small primates."

They combed the perimeters of the warehouses, looking for openings.

"I've found something," said Tem. "It looks like someone tried to hide an exposed vent shaft."

"Excellent, I'm on my way."

"Jon," said Anie, "I've found something too, another vent shaft with the cover missing."

Jona said, "We've got two possibilities. What now?"

"We look at 'em both. Let's go see what Tem found."

They met Tem underneath the vent shaft.

Jon looked up and frowned. "There's no way a human could fit in there," he said.

"Were you thinking about going in after them?"

"We have to find out who and where they are."

Anie said, "I can answer the 'where' part."

Jon turned to look at her. "What?" he began, then looked up to where Anie was pointing.

Along the second-story walkway surrounding the warehouse, dozens of monkeys peered down at them.

Chapter 18

For several long seconds, nobody moved or spoke.

Finally Tem broke the silence. "So..."

As if on cue, the monkeys began to climb down from the walkway, jumping down to the floor of the warehouse with athletic grace.

They spread out and slowly converged on the group. Although they had not made any noise or threatening gestures, Jon was unnerved by the deliberateness of their motions.

As they tightened the circle around them, Jon said in a low voice, "Get your weapons ready."

Then one monkey stepped out from the circle. Jon couldn't be sure, but it might have been the monkey he had chased the previous night.

"There will be no need for weapons here," said the monkey.

For a brief moment, Jon thought he was dreaming again. He quickly looked at the others, who stared at the monkey with the same expression he must have had a second earlier.

"Did that monkey just talk?" asked Jona.

"Please," the monkey continued in a high, resonant voice, "put down your weapons, we are not dangerous."

"Who are you?" said Jon. He was relieved that his voice had not broken when he asked the question.

The monkey's tail flicked back and forth.

"We might ask you the same question."

Jon said, "That's fair. My name is Jon Prospero and I and these people escaped from the Prison several days ago. We're trying..."

Jon was suddenly struck by the absurdity of this whole situation – here he was, about to reveal his plans to go through the center of the planet to a bunch of monkeys.

"Yes?" the monkey prompted.

"We're trying to escape," said Jona.

"By traveling downward?" asked the monkey.

"Yeah," fininshed Jon lamely. He wasn't sure he wanted to reveal any more to these creatures than necessary.

There were high-pitched whispers among the other monkeys. The monkey who stood apart from the group nodded slowly, its tail flicking from side to side.

"Interesting. Why were you imprisoned?" the monkey asked.

Jon debated holding back some information, but before he could answer, Jona said, "We all had run-ins with Medusa Mercantus."

At the mention of Medusa's name, the monkey's tail stopped in mid-flicker, and a new wave of high-pitched whispering erupted among the gathering. Blinking rapidly, the monkey said, "I see."

"My name is Eva Wen Dial, and I am, or rather was, the Chief Engineer of the Imperium Geothermal Project."

The group looked at her.

"The Geothermal Project was conceived a decade ago by the Council of Overseers as a secret mandate. The Council had the foresight to see that the availability of virtually limitless free power would be the foundation of an economic revival of the planet.

"The project was kept a secret because of the very real political repercussions of suddenly making the Power Generation consortium obsolete – there were many very politically powerful and dangerous people that would have...interfered with the project."

"You mean 'sabotaged,'" said Kiala.

Wen Dial said, "Yes."

"So what went wrong?" asked Tem.

"The first several years of the project were successful beyond anyone's dreams. Administrative, coordination, support, supply, and research facilities were built in the Big Cavern in less than two years..."

"You mean 'The Labyrinth.'" said Anie.

Wen Dial made a small snorting sound, "Yes, it had acquired that nickname."

"Once our base was established, the excavations began in earnest. Our seismologists and geologists mapped stable fissures in the tectonic plates we exploited to make the elevator shafts. Sometimes the fissures turned out to be unstable, thus forcing us to drill shafts, which was time-consuming. But as a bonus, we uncovered vast amounts of precious and useful minerals in our excavations."

"We saw them on our way down," said Jon. "They were magnificent."

"The Council was delighted at this new discovery. The project was instantly transformed from a financial risk to one that would pay for itself even if the initial research goal wasn't attained."

"In the third year, we descended steadily down through the crust, excavating support stops, and mining small amounts of the metals."

"Except for medical supplies and food, we were almost completely self-sustainable."

"But when we reached the inner core boundary, we ran into some technical issues – the boundary wasn't consistently equidistant from the center of the core."

"You mean the inner core isn't perfectly spherical," said Tem.

Wen Dial's tail flicked. "Correct. We had to go back to the drawing board. We also had some issues with the intense magnetic flux of the core to deal with, so the project suffered its first real setback."

"As it turns out, a junior level bureaucrat in the Civil Stability group somehow got a copy of the status report, and inflated the health and safety concerns over magnetic pollution..."

Jon said, "Let me guess, the bureaucrat's name was Medusa Mercantus."

"And she had the project shut down," finished Jona.

"Yes, eventually. But in the meantime, we solved both core issues, completed the circumCore tramway, finished connecting all the power conduits – we were mere weeks away from beginning full production tests – maybe a month or two from beginning full production."

"Then Medusa killed the project."

Eva Wen Dial's tail flicked angrily back and forth. "Yes."

Jona couldn't resist any longer. "Um, how did you get to be a monkey?"

Eva Wen Dial blinked rapidly again. "It's a long story."

"Ironically enough, Mercantus herself had included funding for safety and health research. It was an odd request for Civil Stability to make, since normally LifeQualty would have conducted the research, but since the project had been classified 'Secret', Civil Stability had the authority. Medusa commandeered several buildings in the Labyrinth, placing them off limits to us – odd again for what was supposed to be a public health care facility, but again, she had the authority, and the medical treatment our workers were getting was adequate, so I didn't see a problem."

"I didn't think much of the arrangement at the time; after all, it was another necessary part of the greater project. I was soon to regret my inattention."

"On the day we learned that the project was to be shut down, I and most of my staff," she swept her paw toward the other monkeys, "were in conference when Medusa's thugs barged in and took us to her medical labs.

"It was then we learned what she had spent all that money for."

"Mind transference," guessed Tem.

Eva Wen Dial nodded, "Yes. Her geneticists had been experimenting with transferring the consciousness of primates into other primates. I learned that she had also been experimenting on humans."

Jon immediately thought of some of the people in the King's army.

She paused.

"Some of my workers had been lost on excavations, or so we thought. It turns out that they had been kidnapped and used for Medusa's experiments."

"Unsuccessful?" said Kiala softly.

"First experiments generally are unsuccessful. It was horrible; they were worse than mindless. It was horrible to think what nightmare landscapes they were forced to walk through."

"So what happened to you?" asked Jon gently.

Wen Dial again made that sound that Jon took for laughter. "Medusa wanted to keep us alive, but she also needed more human subjects to test. So we all were subject to the transference process."

"It was a spectacular success," she said bitterly.

"What happened to your, uh, human bodies?" asked Anie.

"Supposedly, our bodies are stored somewhere."

"Are they still alive?"

"I don't know."

"Can the mind transference be reversed?" asked Jona.

"Unfortunately, the experimentation never got that far," said Eva Wen Dial. "Medusa's political star was rising. She shut the labs down and abandoned the Labyrinth."

"And you," said Jon.

"And us," agreed Eva Wen Dial.

"What have you been doing since then? How have you managed to live?" asked Kiala.

Wen Dial made the laughing sound again

"It hasn't been a picnic. Fortunately, our monkey hosts were young and strong, and in general, monkeys are not susceptible to human diseases and illnesses, so we have been healthy.

"We continue to excavate a series of tunnels on this level. As we are able, we monitor what goes on above. We kept hoping that one day, someone would come down here with news that Medusa was gone, and that someone would try to help us.

"Every so often, we travel up to the Labyrinth in search of food. Fortunately, we require less food than humans, so we have managed to survive."

One of the monkeys came up to Eva Wen Dial and whispered to her.

Eva Wen Dial looked at Jon, "You said that you had escaped from the Prison?"

"Yes," said Jon.

"It appears they want you back."

"What?" snapped Jona.

"Several heavily-armed prison personnel are on their way down here as we speak."

Jon said, "Are you sure they're from the prison? We also had a run-in with the King of the Labyrinth."

Again the second monkey whispered to Eva Wen Dial.

"No, these are Prison staff, with state-of-the-art weapons. I am told that the Prison staff engaged the King's army and that now the King of the Labyrinth is either dead or in hiding. Prison automata are sweeping the Labyrinth for what's left of the King's army; another group, with humans and automata, just entered an elevator. They should arrive in another few hours."

Tem asked, "But why would they be pursuing us? They threw us in the Labyrinth to begin with."

Jona held up a crystal. "Probably because of this."

They all looked at her.

"When I was a 'guest' of the Warden, I stumbled upon a file that contained correspondences between the Warden and Medusa Mercantus. The file had audio and video records of her bribes, extortions, plans for expanding the Prison... It's a perfect record of her crimes."

Tem let out a low whistle.

Jon said, "I guess we should be going then."

Eva Wen Dial said, "Where will you go? The only option is down."

"That's right," said Tem.

They hurried back to the sleeping area, got their packs and returned to the transport vehicle. Eva Wen Dial and the other monkeys met them there.

As Jon and Tem prepared the transport, Kiala asked Eva Wen Dial, "What will you do?"

"We have very secure hiding places. When you leave, we'll drop the force fields, so the Prison staff will have the blinding storm to contend with. We'll make sure that any traces of your presence are removed. Don't worry about us; we've lived here for years."

Wen Dial examined the transport's cargo area.

"You have heatsuits?"

"Yes."

"With extra power cells?"

"Yes."

"Good, you'll need them. You'll also need shielded communicators. Those you have now will not function near the inner core."

She motioned to one of the other monkeys who ran off into the building.

Jon said, "Thank you. Is there anything..."

"Why don't you come with us?" Anie interrupted him.

Jona added, "You know more about what we'll be facing than anyone. I have the specifications, the blueprints, the disaster plans, but you've been there."

Eva Wen Dial hesitated.

Jon said, "You spoke earlier about being rescued. If you come with us, you increase all our chances of being free again."

"If we succeed, will you promise to help us?" asked Eva Wen Dial.

"Absolutely," said Tem solemnly, as the others nodded their agreement.

Eva Wen Dial turned away from them and shuffled away, lost in thought.

After a few moments, she called to several of her companions, and they spoke quickly in high, hushed tones.

She approached them. "You're right. We've lived here in seclusion and denial for years, digging our tunnels, and waiting. We are dead to the world."

She made a bitter sound. "Nobody's coming for us. Our only hope is to help you."

Jon reached out and touched her shoulder. She put her tiny paw on top of his hand. "Well, if I'm going, then we'll need a few more things."

She instructed several of her companions to get additional gear for her, and they ran off into the tunnels.

They returned presently with several containers holding shielded communicators, and other instruments Jon couldn't identify.

Tem helped them load the containers onto the transport.

Eva said to the group, "Please give me a few minutes to say goodbye to my friends."

"Of course," Jon said.

They got into the transport, and Jon moved a short distance from the group of monkeys who surrounded Eva Wen Dial. They were all swaying and hugging each other, and making low moaning noises.

"They don't think she's coming back," said Kiala.

"They've been living in fear for years," said Jon. "Maybe Eva's decision will give them the courage to hope."

"Or make them feel totally abandoned," said Jona.

Tem said, "I've got a really good feeling about this. After all, she's the one who designed the station, right? She's gotta know about what's up ahead."

"Let's hope so," said Jona.

After saying her goodbyes, Eva Wen Dial came up to the transport. Jon opened the door for her, and she asked, "Is there room for more of us?"

Jon looked at Tem and said, "I don't know – how many more want to come with us?"

"Three have volunteered."

Tem looked in the back and said, "I think we can fit in three more. Hop in."

He helped load more supplies into the cargo area, and Eva Wen Dial and her three companions climbed on board.

"We can do introductions on the way. How long before the elevator lands?"

"Approximately forty minutes," said one of the three newcomers.

They approached the forcefield that had kept the storm contained in the outer area. Eva produced a small handheld tablet from her tunic and touched an icon. Designed to fit a human hand, the device looked more like a data tablet in her small, delicate paws.

"The force-field will deactivate in ten seconds," Eva said.

"What about your companions back there?" asked Anie worriedly.

"They're already safely inside, thank you," said the monkey calmly.

When the forcefield finally dropped, the transport sped off toward the elevator. Jona asked Eva, "Can you unlock the Elevator?"

The monkey looked up at her with its wide eyes and said, "You can do it, if you prefer."

"OK. I've done them this far."

"Yes you have," said the monkey.

As the transport approached the elevator, the doors began to open, letting in a swirl of dust and grit. Jon backed the transport in, and Jona closed the doors.

Eva said, "If you'll allow me, I can show you some of the overrides that will give us some additional speed."

Eva showed Jona how to tweak the elevator's governors to gain additional speed. When Jona applied the changes, they all could feel the elevator descending faster.

Eva turned to her companions. "Now I would like to introduce Lim Atal, our chief geophysicist." Atal was slightly bigger than Wen Dial, and his coat was streaked with white. "I am honored to be here with you," he said in a slightly lower voice that Eva's. "I have to confess, though, that I'm more than a little apprehensive."

At this everyone laughed. Anie reached out and patted his arm. "Join the club."

"And," Eva continued, "this is Rel Wodu, my capable assistant engineer. Rel supervised the day-to-day operations of the first several years of construction. He was a miracle-worker."

If monkeys could blush, Rel would have. He said, "Just doing my job."

"And last, I'd like to introduce Pir Wen Dial, my husband."

"Your husband?" said Jona before she could stop herself.

Pir said, "I couldn't let her go off on this joyride without me."

The elevator continued downward.

Chapter 19

The next level was in much better shape than the one above, with all its structures intact but silent. The group decided to press on, and descend one more level before stopping to rest.

"Eva, are you still in contact with your companions?" Jon asked.

"Yes," she answered.

"What happened with the Prison guards who were after us?"

"They searched the building, but, of course, found nothing. However they are continuing to pursue us."

"They didn't discover any of your companions, did they?" asked Kiala.

"No," Eva said.

"We've gotten pretty good at hiding," said Rel.

"What will we find at this next level?" asked Jon.

Lim Atal said, "Each level is pretty much like the one above it, except for the topmost level, of course. Cargo bays, crew quarters, admin building."

"Can we stop and rest here?"

"I don't think that would be a good idea," said Pir. "The Prison force has never pursued prisoners this far down before."

"Have any other prisoners ever made it this far?" asked Tem.

"No, you get the prize."

Jon said, "So the plan is to put as much distance between us and the Prison guards. That means we can't stop on any levels for any length of time."

Tem groaned, "No more rest stops, no more cots?"

"I'm afraid not," said Eva.

"Is there any way to sabotage the elevators?" Jon asked.

Eva said, "As much as I'd like to consider that option given our present circumstances, I'm afraid that would be impossible. An elevator malfunction was our worst nightmare when we were building the station."

"Understandable."

"The best we can do would be to interfere with the elevator's command processing, and we're already doing that."

"Right now, we have a six hour lead. Let's try to increase that if we can."

They spent the next several days going down elevator after elevator, only staying on each level long enough to eat and take care of sanitation needs. They took turns sleeping on the transport.

"How much farther to the core?" asked Kiala.

"Two more levels," Rel said, "then we should be able to do something about our pursuers."

"What do you mean?" asked Jon.

Eva said, "We'll be at the deepest level of the station. From that point, we'll need to wear heatsuits until we begin going upward again. We join the circumCore tramway there."

"And then we disable the tramway," Rel said.

"Rel..." Eva warned.

"Not permanently, of course. Just enough to buy us more time."

On the way down, Eva had taught Jona how to access the more advanced functions of the elevator control system.

"Um, Eva?" said Jona worriedly.

"Yes?"

"You said that we had tweaked the elevator to descend at the fastest safe rate?"

"Yes, we've been traveling like that for several levels."

"Well, it looks like our Prison buddies are cheating – they seem to be exceeding the maximum safe descent speed."

Eva took Jona's tablet. In her tiny paws the tablet looked like an oversized book held by a child.

"You're right. At the increased descent speed, they might catch up to us before we can get to the tramway."

"Then let's go faster," said Anie.

"I'm reluctant to..." began Eva, but Pir cut her off.

"Dear, we can't afford to be caught. With the evidence Jona has against Medusa, I'm sure we'll be killed on sight. I say let's drop as fast as this thing will let us."

"You're right, of course." she agreed.

"This is our chance to get our life back." He gently squeezed her paw.

"OK," said Jona, "do I push it to its real maximum?"

Eva shrugged and said, "Do it."

As they descended faster, Rel said, "I hope the dampers work at this speed."

"They're working for our pursuers. They'll work for us," said Eva.

Pir said, "We need to get into our heatsuits before we get to this level. The temperature will spike rapidly once we leave the elevator. Also, your communicators won't work down here. You'll have to use the shielded ones. They should be in the back, along with the heatsuits."

When they finally descended to the tramway level, the dampers worked just fine, and the transport rolled out of the elevator.

The humans were totally unprepared for what they saw next: the brilliant, seething, molten core of the planet right in front of them. Enclosed by unimaginably strong force-fields, this level of the station literally floated on the molten sea.

Protected by their heatsuits, the humans could only gasp in wonder.

Finally, Tem managed to say, "This is unbelievable."

In a heatsuit several sizes too big for her, Eva said, "Yes, it is breathtaking. I haven't been down here since the level was built, and I'd forgotten how magnificent it is."

Looking at her heatsuit power reading, she said, "We need to hurry to the trams. Hopefully, they'll be functional."

"And if not?" asked Tem.

"Then you'll get a crash course in high-temperature magnetic core tramaway repair."

"Please don't say 'crash'", said Kiala, gripping her armrest with white knuckles.

Chapter 20

The transport sped down the corridor toward the distant tramway. On all sides a force-field held back the searing heat. The core itself pulsed a few hundred feet below them.

As they drove, Eva said, "This is the only level that was never permanently inhabited. Several crew spent week-long shifts down here – with three-times-normal pay – but no one was allowed to spend more than that. The environment was just too dangerous."

"Were there any...eruptions... of the core? I mean, could there be?" asked Tem.

"There's always that risk, but no, there never was an occurrence."

They approached the tramway stop. The bullet-shaped tram stood on a gleaming pedestal.

Human and monkey got out of the transport. The air shimmered around them.

Eva said, "Quickly, let's get moving."

The group grabbed everything they could carry out of the transport, and hurried toward the tram control area.

Eva approached the opening and keyed in the passcode. The door opened and they all bundled in.

After they were all inside, Rel sat down at the control console, looking just like a tiny monkey playing at being a control operator. His tiny paws danced over the displays. After a few seconds he looked up.

"I've got good news and bad news."

"Oh boy," said Jona.

Eva said, "Bad news first."

"We can't leave right now."

"Why not," said Eva.

"The contact layer underneath the tram, the part that touches the razor thin magnetic field generated by the track, is flaking off – theoretically, we could still use the tram, but chances are very good we'd get stranded half way to our next destination."

"That would be a bad thing," said Jona.

Rel continued, "The layer really wasn't designed to last years anyhow, so I wouldn't consider the failure a design flaw."

Eva snorted, "Once an engineer, always an engineer. OK, what's the good news?"

"There's a backup tram that has an undamaged contact layer."

"So, what's the plan?"

"We switch out the good tram car for the bad, and leave the bad one for our pursuers."

"Knowing they could become stranded if they follow us?" asked Anie.

"We could leave them a note," snapped Jona.

"We'll discuss the ethics later. Let's do it," said Jon.

With Jona and Tem's help, Rel switched the trams and had the backup tram powered up and ready to go in twenty minutes.

"All aboard," said Rel.

Eva said, "Rel, can you engage some lockouts so our pursuers won't have the chance to use the defective tram?"

Rel said, "I can, but there would be no guarantee that they wouldn't defeat the overrides – but even if they do, that would buy us some time. Hold on."

Anie said, "I'm still concerned about putting them in mortal danger."

Rel answered, "If it makes you feel better, the tram will probably fail within a few miles of this station. Protected by their heatsuits, they can safely walk back here. OK?"

The monkey engaged the lockouts and switched the control console to automatic.

The group loaded all the cargo they had been carrying into the tram. Once they and the cargo were aboard, there wasn't much room to spare.

"OK, let's go," said Eva.

Rel disengaged the locks holding the tram, and the vehicle slowly began to move down the tunnel, gradually increasing in speed.

"Open up your heatsuit helmets and cut your power. Let's conserve as much as we can. I don't know if there will be any functioning rechargers ahead." said Eva.

Tem began to climb out of his suit when Eva warned him, "I wouldn't recommend taking the suits off, though. The tram might lose power or have another malfunction, and the temperature in here could climb hundreds of degrees in a matter of seconds."

Tem quickly put his suit back on.

"I'm cool," he said sheepishly.

"At least your suits fit you," Lim complained, waving a sleeve that was at least a foot longer than his arm.

For the next few hours, they sped over an ocean of molten lava.

"Magnificent, isn't it?" said Eva.

"It's so beautiful," agreed Kiala.

At last, they arrived at the next stop and changed trams. As before, Rel disabled their old tram. Eva and Jona monitored the system for any sign of their pursuers.

"Are we still being chased?" Jon asked.

"Don't know," Jona said. "The magnetic interference down here is playing havoc with the cameras."

Eva said, "The cameras down here are notoriously unreliable due to the flux fields. We'll try in another hour to see if we can get some better images."

"Let's assume the worst, and keep moving as fast as we can."

"That would be prudent," agreed Eva.

———

They arrived at the second tram stop without incident. Rel rechecked the tram's systems, while the rest of the group headed toward the control room.

Jon said, "Let's try to find out if we're still being followed."

Eva and Jona were already busy booting up consoles and computers.

"That's why we're here. All the electronics here should be hardened, and they've been either completely inactive or in sleep mode since the work here was stopped."

After several minutes, Jona made a huffing noise.

"What is it?" asked Kiala.

Eva said calmly, "We're still being followed. A tram left the last stop about three hours ago. Estimated arrival is one hour."

Jona examined the display and said, "Wait a minute, this doesn't look right. Look at the tram's change in position."

Eva frowned and said, "Just a minute, please." She tapped out a series of commands on the handheld pad she carried.

"It seems that our pursuers have also discovered a way to increase the tram's speed to one hundred and twenty percent of its rated maximum."

"Which means?" asked Tem.

"Which means," said Jona, "they'll be here in thirty-five minutes."

Kiala said, "Let's get out of here."

"Wait a minute," said Jon. "If they've found a way to increase their speed, they'll catch up to us in what, less than an hour?"

Jona said, "Something like that."

"So it won't do any good to run. We need to stop them."

Eva looked at Pir and Rel, "Any ideas?" She looked at Rel and added, "that won't permanently damage the tramline, please."

There was an uncomfortably long pause.

Finally, Pir said, "An EMP ring."

Rel nodded enthusiastically, "That would do it."

"What's an EMP ring?" asked Tem.

Pir said, "It's a large ring used for generating controlled electromagnetic pulses. The inside of the ring is lined with pulse emitters, and the outside of the ring generates a damping field, confining the pulse to the area inside the ring. It doesn't have many practical applications – mostly it's used for testing hardened electronic systems in controlled conditions."

"It's also been useful in urban warfare," Eva added. She frowned at Pir.

Tem said, "I say we have a practical application right now."

Jona asked, "Is one down here?"

Pir scurried off toward a storage bay.

Jon asked. "If there is one, what's the plan?"

Rel said, "We move several miles down the tube, stop, engage the ring behind us, then take off again. Our pursuers pass through the ring, the electromagnetic pulse disables the tram's systems, and the tram coasts to a stop.

"The pursuers will then have to walk back to this station. Depending on how far out we strand them, it could take them a few hours to get back."

Eva said, "We'll place the ring four miles out. That should enable them to return here in an hour or so. They should have enough reserve in their heatsuits to do that. I don't want to kill anybody."

Eva looked toward the storage bay. Pir was heading toward them, driving a maintenance cart full of equipment.

Pir stopped the vehicle at the rear of the tram, jumped down and shuffled quickly up to them.

"We're in luck, I've got everything we need. Rel, Tem, help me load it into the tram?"

Tem picked up two small, flat boxes. "What are these?"

"Triggers. We'll place several sets of them a few hundred yards in front of the ring. The tram goes by the first trigger and the EMP ring begins pulsing.

"How long can the ring send out a pulse?"

"Three minutes. Don't worry, at the speed the tram will be traveling, there's no way that it could stop before it passes through the ring."

They loaded the ring onto the tram and left the station, heading out to a point four miles down the tramline. Jon and Pir sealed up their heatsuits, got out, and unloaded the ring components.

Kiala asked Jona, "How long do we have?"

Jona said, "About twenty minutes. Plenty of time. No worries. Can we hurry this up?"

Pir handed Jon the triggers. "Pay attention. Take these and head down the tunnel about two hundred yards. Place the triggers every ten yards of so, working back toward us. Put them as high on the side supports as you can reach. And this is important – make sure before you attach them, you're on our side of the trigger. Once they make contact with the tunnel supports, they'll become armed."

"Whatever you do, once you've set them, don't trip them!"

"Understood," Jon said, and took off at a fast trot back toward the station.

While Jon set the triggers, Tem and Pir assembled the ring.

"OK, ready to go," said Pir, as Jon came running back toward the tram.

"Let's get out of here. Go, go go." said Jona.

Jona asked, "Will we be able to tell when the device is tripped?"

Pir said, "Not until we get to our destination."

Anie had been unusually pensive during the entire trip. She said brightly, "If they don't catch up to us before we reach the next station, we'll know."

"True."

As they raced forward, Jona and Eva tried to patch into the station's communications system, but the magnetic interference wouldn't allow a stable connection. The best they managed to get were some grainy, inconclusive pictures and a lot of static.

They arrived at their destination, Station B, and quickly made their way to the control room. Eva and Jona again restarted the silent equipment and checked the logs for any sign of tram activity other than their own.

Eva said, "Another tram did leave the station, and, yes, the EMP ring did activate. Beside our tram, there are no records of tram activity beyond that point."

"We did it!" said Kiala enthusiastically.

"So it would seem," said Eva.

"We still need to keep moving," said Jon.

"Agreed," said Eva.

"We're safe for now, aren't we?" asked Tem. "Can't we rest here?"

Eva said, "Under normal circumstances, the answer would be 'No.' Under these circumstances, the answer is a very emphatic 'No.' If they've pursued you this far, they're determined indeed. All we've done is slow them down."

Jona punched Tem in the arm. "Come on, you can sleep when you're dead."

"That's what I'm afraid of."

"I have an idea," said Rel. "Let's send the tram on to the next station. If somebody is monitoring the trams, whoever is following us just might pursue it."

"Or they may split up into two groups," added Jona. "That's not a bad idea."

"But first things first," she said. "Let's get the elevator going. If we can't, we'll need to go to the next station ourselves."

Jon asked Eva, "Is there a vehicle we can commandeer on this level?"

Eva looked at Pir, who replied, "Not big enough to carry us all. We'll have to go up to the next level."

They hurried toward the elevator entrance, taking one last look at the spectacular sight of the inner core through the protective forcefields.

At the entrance, Jona popped the access panel, poked her head inside for several seconds, then pronounced the hardware undamaged.

Using her own pad, Eva opened the door, and the group hurried into the elevator.

Rel went back to set the tram's autopilot, and the group watched the tram move slowly away.

As Rel scampered back, Eva said, "Going up," and started the sequence to carry them up to the next level.

The ride up was uneventful, and Tem even stretched out on the floor.

"Are you going to sleep down there?" asked Anie.

"Yep." said Tem, and eventually the rest of the group followed his lead and either sat against the walls or lay down. The monkeys whispered quietly to themselves.

Eventually, they could feel the car decelerating, and knew that they would be arriving at the next level at any time. Finally, they felt a small jolt, and then the car stopped.

As everyone stood up, Eva opened the door.

This level, like all the others, felt abandoned and deserted.

Eva said, "We can now remove our heatsuits – we won't need them again."

She motioned to her left. "There should be a storage bay down this corridor. Let's split up into two groups – one group can look for a transport and the other can look for supplies in the support building. Meet at the support building entrance in an hour?"

"Forty-five minutes." said Jon. "We need to keep moving."

"OK, forty-five minutes, then," agreed Eva.

Jona said, "We should now be able to track them if they get up this far."

"That would make me feel a lot better."

Tem said, "OK, let's go plunder. Time's a wastin'."

Jon, Tem, Anie, Lim, Pir, and Rel found several transports in the bay, but upon closer examination, all but one needed repair. They loaded up the functioning transport with additional fuel cells, and made their way back to the support building.

Jona, Eva, Lim, and Kiala swept through the support building, gathering food and water supplies.

They loaded the supplies into the new transport and headed toward the up elevator entrance, and continued their journey upward.

"Any sign of our pursuers?" Jon asked.

"None – no activity at the core station."

"Maybe we could risk stopping for a longer period at the next level," said Tem hopefully.

"Maybe," said Eva. "but I'd feel safer if we had several levels between us and them."

"Me too," said Jona.

They continued traveling upward, arriving at the next level on schedule.

This level, like the others, was lonely and deserted.

The group decided to go directly to the up elevator and continue their ascent.

Anie said, "I noticed that we're not going through any caverns." Jon realized that she was right – the elevator cage traveled upward though a shaft, but they had not seen any of the amazing caverns they had seen on their way down.

Lim said, "That's right – this area of the planet had a different tectonic structure that the other main shaft. This drilldown was actually easier than the first – although we didn't find any caverns, the rock was less dense and the strata was consistently stable. Boring – just the way we like it."

"I always thought drilling was boring work," joked Tem.

The monkeys just looked at him, but Jona said, "Don't make me come over there."

The next level was considerably larger than the ones below it.

Eva said, "This was the base level for our effort to get to the core for this shaft. If we wanted to rest for several hours, this would be a good place."

They agreed to rest for four hours, then continue on.

They entered the support building, found the dorm area, and stretched out on the first cots they had seen in days.

Eva and Jona set alarms that would alert them if anyone came through either the up or down elevator entrance, or any part of the building.

Reassured that they were relatively safe, Jon sank down on a cot and was asleep within seconds.

Chapter 21

They got three hours of sleep before the automatic alarms signaled that their pursuers were again approaching.

Groaning, Tem reached for his shoes. "How long until we get to the surface?" he asked.

"Two more levels; then we'll be at the surface staging area for this shaft," said Eva.

The group continued their upward journey.

Upon their arrival at the second level, Jon hardly allowed the doors to open completely before he raced to the final up elevator that would bring them to the surface.

"We're in the home stretch," said Kiala brightly.

As the doors to the elevator shut behind them, there was almost a festive atmosphere in the transport. Only Jon remained aloof.

"What are you going to do when you get out?" Tem asked Jona.

"Oh, I don't know, probably get a hotel and take a long, hot, bath."

Then, realizing the monkeys had become very quiet, Tem said, "Well, the first thing I'd do would be, to, uh..." He stopped talking.

Kiala looked at Eva and her companions. "The first thing we'll do is everything we can to help you once this is over."

Eva's tail flicked back and forth, but she remained silent, lost in thought.

"The first thing we'll do is get Jona's crystal to the authorities," said Jon.

Eventually, Pir said, "At least we'll be better off on the surface."

Several minutes later, Jona said, "We're not moving," She checked her tablet.

"What?" said Jon.

"The elevator is no longer moving," confirmed Eva.

"Well, can we override whatever it is they're doing?" said Tem.

"I'm trying," said Jona impatiently. "We've been locked out."

Just then, the elevator shuddered.

"What was that?" asked Anie.

"We're going back down."

Eva said, "We have to get out."

"What?" they all said in unison.

"We have to get out of the elevator."

She thought quickly. "Maintenance tunnels."

"There are maintenance tunnels that run parallel to the elevator shaft. We'll have to climb, but I don't see any other option. There's a trapdoor on top of the elevator car. I suggest we hurry."

They climbed on top of the transport. Tem and Jon opened the trapdoor, and helped everyone up.

The view up the shaft was dizzying.

Just as Tem climbed onto the top of the car, the car shuddered again and began picking up speed.

"Oh boy," said Kiala.

Eva said, "Step off and grab the access ladder. Do it now!"

"I'll go first," said Rel, and deftly grabbed a rung of the ladder. He waved to them as the car continued to move downward.

Without a word, Anie jumped next and grabbed a rung. She was several feet below Rel, who had already started climbing.

"It's going too fast now," said Jona fearfully.

"No, you can make it. Go! " urged Eva.

Jona stepped toward the edge of the car, took a deep breath, and lunged toward the ladder.

Lim went next, followed by Kiala, Pir, and Tem. Only Jon and Eva were left.

Eva said, "Go right after me, OK?" She leapt off the car toward the ladder. The car was moving so fast now Jon couldn't tell if she had grabbed onto the ladder or not.

The ladder was now moving so fast that Jon couldn't make out individual rungs. He took a breath, flexed his legs, and jumped.

Chapter 22

Jon hit the ladder with a thud, and for a sickening second, grabbed only air. He scrambled wildly, then his left hand found a rung. He clamped down with all his strength, grimacing with pain as his shoulder threatened to leave its socket. He grabbed the same rung with his right hand as his feet found the rungs beneath him. After saying a silent prayer of thanks, he summoned the courage to look up. Several dozen feet above him, he saw Eva peering down at him.

"Are you OK?" she asked.

"Fine, thanks. Couldn't be better. You?"

"There's a maintenance accessway several hundred feet above us. Rel should already be there."

Eva called out, "Slow and steady, everybody can make it."

Using his communicator, Jon checked in with the group.

After an eternity of nerve-wracking climbing, the group had all collapsed onto the catwalk in front of the accessway.

Rubbing his arm muscles, Tem said, "If I never see a ladder again, it'll be too soon."

Eva said, "That's unfortunate, because we may need to climb again to reach the surface if the maintenance elevators are unusable."

"I can climb some more," he said quickly.

They entered the accessway and found the elevator Eva had mentioned.

"Is it functional?" asked Jon.

Jona said, "We'll know in a minute."

Eva added, "This set of elevators was intentionally set on a different command circuit. As long as the mechanisms are undamaged, it's unlikely that whoever hijacked the main elevator even knows about this one."

Jon said, "Our pursuers have managed to surprise us before."

"Point taken," replied Eva.

Jona and Eva confirmed that the elevator was working, and they all crowded in and continued upward.

Rel said, "The next stop should be the surface. We should be there in under an hour."

"Happy," said Tem.

As Rel had predicted, the elevator arrived at the surface fifty-seven minutes later. Before the doors opened, Jon said, "Nobody get out or make a sound until we've had a chance to look around."

"Agreed," said Eva.

Jon stepped silently out of the car into a dark corridor. A few rays of light seeped in through closed up windows high overhead. This building had obviously been unused for years.

Jon quickly scanned the area, and satisfied that all was safe, motioned for the others to follow.

"OK, which way out?" he asked Eva.

Eva pointed to a set of large doors across the room. "Through those doors are the loading docks."

They made their way quickly across the room, sending eddies of dust up as they passed.

Pir disengaged the lock and opened the door.

On the other side stood Medusa Mercantus and several dozen heavily-armed security guards.

Chapter 23

"Well, Mr. Prospero, it took you long enough to get here." Medusa smiled and casually walked toward them. Behind her, stood the Prison Director of Security and the Prison Overwarden.

"On the other hand, I do have to thank you." Medusa said smoothly. "I have been assured for years by these – gentlemen – that our facility was escape-proof, and you have generously shown us that it's not. Isn't that right, Overwarden?"

The Overwarden studied his shoes.

"Oh, don't look so sad," She laughed.

She stopped. "Where are the others?" she asked abruptly.

"What others?" asked Jon.

The Directory of Security said, "I...I don't know."

"Seal off the area," Medusa snapped. "Find them. Now!"

Several guards immediately hurried off.

Jon looked around. Jona, Eva, Pir, Lim, and Rel had disappeared.

"Where did they go, Jon?" she asked menacingly

"How should I know? You seem to have all the answers."

"You enjoy taking chances, don't you." she sneered.

"What harm could I do?"

"Oh, you've already caused me trouble. People usually regret causing me trouble."

Jon said, "Why are you doing this? Why not turn the geothermal station on?"

Medusa looked around. "Oh, I plan to, in due time. But first things first. I need to consolidate my power on the Imperium Council of Overseers. You see, political power precedes industrial power. If the fools had made virtually unlimited geothermal power available, there would have been a commercial renaissance, and my power base, my political power base, would have evaporated. Nothing makes a zealot like misery and an object of hatred. Oh, things are going to get a lot worse around here before they get better." She smiled again.

Just then, a small, insistent voice whispered in Jon's ear. "Jon, slowly step back two paces."

It was Eva. Jon had completely forgotten about his communicator.

He slowly shuffled back in line with the others. Then, a shimmering appeared inches in front of him, separating them from Medusa and her guards.

"What is this?" snarled Medusa. "Guards, kill them now. Fire!"

The guards open fire on Jon and the others, but their weapons fire bounced off the force-field, causing them to duck to avoid the ricochets.

As he watched, the force-field moved toward Medusa and the guards, effectively corralling them in a corner of the warehouse.

From the opposite end of the warehouse, a transport roared into life and moved toward them. Rel waved at them from the driver's seat.

"Get in!"

The group piled into the vehicle, and Rel spun the transport around and headed toward the far exit.

"Is everybody OK?" asked Eva. "Pir remembered that this facility was used to do the initial testing of the force-fields used for the station. It was fortunate the equipment still worked."

"I'll say," said Tem. "I thought we were goners."

"We're not free yet," said Jona. "Look."

Behind them, at the far end of the warehouse, security guards were running toward them and shooting.

"Everybody hold on," Rel said, and raced toward the doors.

"Wait, wait, slow down. Give me time to open the doors." said Eva. Rel scraped the sides of the transport as it passed through the doorway. At last they were outside.

"Rel, take the next left," said Pir.

At the other end of the building, Medusa's troops ran to their vehicles.

"They're coming after us," Tem shouted.

"You think?" said Jona.

"I'm going as fast as I can," said Rel. He turned left onto the road Pir had indicated, barely slowing down.

Pir said, "We're heading toward a main surface transport hub. If we can make it, we can get lost in the general traffic flow."

"Sounds good to me," said Jon.

They sped down the road.

"Turn right at the next intersection," said Pir.

Again, barely slowing down, Rel turned into the new road and accelerated to top speed. The road curved gently to the right.

Jon checked behind them for signs of pursuit.

"Oh, no," squeaked Rel.

They all turned around.

About a hundred meters ahead of them was a heavily-fortified roadblock.

Rel slammed on the brakes and the transport came to a stop.

Jon looked back to see Medusa's troops coming up behind them.

They were in an artificial canyon; high walls on either side of the road, and no doors or windows at ground level. They were trapped.

Chapter 24

"What now?" asked Tem.

"Do we have any weapons?" asked Jona.

"We can't win a firefight," said Jon.

Just then, a familiar voice spoke from their communicators, "Jon, get everybody out of the transport and gather in front of the vehicle. Do it now."

Jon paused, trying to identify the voice. "Syd? Syd Shining?"

"Hey partner, get a move on – everybody out of the vehicle. Now! I'll pick you up in thirty-seven seconds."

Jon looked at the others.

"You heard the man. Go!"

They all got out of the transport and huddled down beneath the front fender. Medusa's troops came closer.

Eva pointed to an object in the sky, approaching very quickly.

"There he is."

It was a cargo shuttle, very fast, and small enough to land in the enclosed area. As soon as Medusa's troops saw where the shuttle was heading, they opened fire on it.

Syd Shining made a power landing ten meters in front of the transport, and moments later, opened the cargo doors.

His amplified voice boomed from the shuttle. "Run!"

The group sprinted toward the shuttle.

Syd had positioned the shuttle to protect them from the troops in front of the transport, but by now, the group that had been following them was close enough to shoot at them.

As Eva ran toward the shuttle, an energy blast hit her in the back. Crying out, she fell.

Jon and Tem both looked back and stopped.

Jon yelled, "I'll get her."

Tem nodded, and continued on toward the shuttle.

Jon ran back and picked Eva up, then sprinted toward the shuttle. Tem secured everybody else on board, and when Jon climbed aboard with Eva, he slammed the cargo doors shut.

Medusa's troops ran toward the shuttle, firing steadily.

"Syd, we're all in!"

Syd gunned the engines and the shuttle instantly jumped ten meters in the air, throwing Jon and Tem to the floor.

"Hang on!"

"Now he tells us," shouted Tem.

As soon as he was clear of the tallest building, Syd accelerated away at right angles from the two groups of Medusa's troops. Soon the shuttle was beyond the weapon's firing distance.

Tem helped Jon up. He still held the unconscious Eva.

Pir and Rel unstrapped themselves from their seats and hurried over to see her.

"Is she OK?" Pir said, his voice trembling.

Jon said, "It looks like the shot didn't hit her squarely. She's suffered a pretty bad burn, and she'll be sore for a few days, but I think she'll be fine."

Pir hugged his wife.

Eva opened her eyes, looked up at Pir, and asked, "We made it?"

He stroked her fur and said, "Yes, we made it."

Jon made his way to the cockpit. Syd Shining sat in the pilot seat, grinning from ear to ear.

Jon grabbed his shoulder heartily and sat down in the co-pilots seat.

"Syd! It's good to see you. I thought you were dead. What happened?"

Syd looked slyly over at his friend, and said, "I thought so too; but that explosion knocked a huge piece of reinforced insulation down on top of me, which saved me from the rest of the blast. The blast blew out the part of the outer wall, so I slipped out of the building before they could find me."

"Have you talked to my wife?"

Keeping his eyes on the controls, Syd said, "Lara's fine. We're on our way to meet her right now."

Jon sank back in his seat and closed his eyes.

"That's great. So what's the plan now?"

Syd looked down at his instruments. "Long story short, the Imperium Council has been, shall we say, fully informed of Medusa's activities, and outside of the local troops she has with her in the field right now, she's doesn't have a lot of friends in the Council anymore."

"Her allies have been working overtime distancing themselves from her. Her authority has been taken away, and by now she's been classified a fugitive."

Jona tapped Jon on the shoulder and handed him the data crystal containing Medusa's correspondence with the Warden.

"Here's more evidence for the Council."

Sys said, "Excellent."

Jon looked out the window. "Where are we going?"

"The Imperium Council."

A few minutes later, they arrived at the Imperium Council complex and landed in a secure area.

A welcoming party was there to greet them, including Lara, a medical group and several Council members.

As soon as the cargo shuttle landed, Jon jumped out onto the landing field and ran to Lara.

She hugged him tightly and said, "I was so worried about you."

Jon said, "I'm glad you got my message."

As they walked arm-in-arm toward the building, Aron Matsumi, GroupLeader of Imperium Infrastructure, and a member of the Council came up to greet them.

"Mr. Prospero, glad you made it back." They shook hands.

"Happy to be here, Councilor. We have some, um, people, who need medical attention."

Medtechs placed Eva on a stretcher. Pir stayed by her side.

"People?" Matsumi stammered.

"It's a long story," said Jon.

Trying to regain his composure, Matsumi said, "I look forward to hearing it."

Jon handed the data crystal to the Councilor. "I think this will be of interest to the Council."

Matsumi cleared his throat and said, "I'm sure it is, and we look forward to hearing your testimony. But, be assured, we've already begun an investigation into the activities of *former* GroupLeader Medusa Mercantus."

Chapter 25

GroupLeader Jon Prospero walked into his office, sat down at his desk to scan his daily meeting schedule, and groaned.

"I need a break already," he said.

Two chimes sounded and a holographic image of his appointment scheduler appeared in front of him.

"GroupLeader?"

"Yes, Eema?"

"Your 9:00 appointment is here."

Jon glanced at his schedule, "Umm."

"The geothermal project update?"

Jon frowned. "Right. Of course. Send him in please?"

Eema said, "It's a 'her', sir."

Jon sighed. "Sorry, send *her* in please?"

A striking older woman entered his office. Although she must have been well into her late middle age, she moved with the grace and poise of an athlete. Jon found himself almost intimidated by her attractiveness.

Jon stood and extended his hand. "I'm Jon Prospero, it's good to..."

The woman smiled broadly and reached out to hug him.

"Jon, it's so good to see you again!"

Taken aback, Jon stiffened and said, "I'm sorry, do I know you?"

The woman grinned and said, "I'm Eva Wen Dial."

Relieved, Jon hugged her back and said, "Oh! It's good to see you again too. You look.....great!"

He cleared his throat. "Please, have a seat."

He added, "I'm sorry I haven't kept up with you. Right now, well, I'm just trying to keep my head above water."

Eva said, "No apology necessary. It's all right. I understand." She smiled. "I've been fairly busy myself."

"So tell me, where to begin?"

She settled back in the chair.

"As you can see, they found our human bodies in one of the underground labs. We, our bodies, I mean, were perfectly preserved in steady sleep, a sort of artificially induced coma. Reviving the team was a simple matter."

"So, you have no memory of being a monkey."

"That's right."

"Probably a good thing," mused Jon.

"Actually, she...I kept an exhaustive journal of her..my experiences underground. It's sometimes unnerving to read." She looked out the window.

"I can imagine," said Jon.

"Apparently," she continued, "you were quite the hero down there."

Jon blushed. "Well, I think everybody was pretty extraordinary. Um, what happened to...um."

"The monkey?"

He nodded.

She took a deep breath. "When they began to revive me, "I", the monkey, was looking at my human body on a table in the lab, and when "I" awoke in my own body, I was "me" again, looking at the monkey."

She held up her hand and gazed at her palm.

"And the monkey, where "I" had been seconds before, was now just an ordinary monkey. A very sweet and docile creature, we've made arrangements for it to be cared for."

"And the others?"

"All fine. All had the same experience."

"Do you feel any different?" asked Jon.

Eva paused. "If I didn't have her...my journal, nothing would be any different. But to read her...my words, it's just, well, I'm still dealing with it."

Jon said, "I understand. If you ever want to talk about it..."

Eva smiled. "Thanks, I'll keep that invitation open. Does Lara like spaghetti? Pir makes excellent spaghetti."

Jon patted him stomach and said, "Oh, we both like spaghetti. We'll bring the dessert."

Jon looked down at his notes. "As far as the project goes, do you need anything?"

Eva said, "No, everything is going smoothly. We should be ready to go live on schedule next month.

"By the way, I'm very grateful for your office loaning me two excellent consultants for the project. It's been great fun working with Jona and Kiala in a less, shall we say, stressful, situation.

Jon chuckled. "Well, after Jona convinced me she had given up her life of crime, I knew she would make a great addition to our team. And both she and Kiala had unique on-the-job training for the assignment.

He added, "I do have a great staff. I just wish I could have been more personally involved."

Eva smiled and stood up. "Delegation is the secret to avoiding insanity."

Well, I've got to get back to the project. It was wonderful to see you again."

Jon hugged her again. "You too."

———————

Two chimes sounded in his ear.

"GroupLeader?"

"Yes, Eema?"

"Your presence is requested at the sentencing of Medusa Mercantus."

"Thank you." He touched a flashing icon on his desktop and Eema's image was replaced by a courtroom in the Imperium Council annex. Representatives from all branches of the Imperium Council sat in judgment.

Wearing his judicial robes, GroupLeader Aron Matsumi acknowledged Jon's virtual presence with a nod.

"Bring the prisoner in." A guard opened a side door, and Medusa Mercantus shuffled into the courtroom. Her hands and feet were restrained and she wore standard prison-issue brown coveralls.

Her team of lawyers followed her, looking none too happy.

The crowd in the courtroom whispered loudly as she sat down and glared at the Council.

Matsumi cleared his throat and began to read. "Medusa Mercantus, you have been charged, tried, and convicted of the following crimes: forgery of government documents, theft of government property and funds, and kidnapping thousands of Imperium citizens."

It is the ruling of this court, that you be sentenced to twenty-five years incarceration in the underground prison you helped create."

"I do not recognize your authority here," she spat.

Matsumi said calmly, "Then you'll have plenty of time to learn. Do all GroupLeaders in attendance approve and sanction this sentence?"

Jon reached forward and voted 'Yes.'

After a few seconds, Matsumi consulted his tablet. "The GroupLeader vote is unanimous. The sentence will be carried out."

Mercantus stood and cried out, "I demand to speak."

Matsumi regarded her and said, "Your time for demanding things here has passed."

She continued to splutter as the guards led her out of courtroom, Masumi rose and said, "This proceeding is now concluded."

Jon dropped the connection, stretched, and tapped the intercom.

"Eema, what do I need to be doing now?"

"You have pending approval of the relocation/restitution agreement between the citizens wrongly imprisoned by Mercantus."

"Also, you have a meeting with Director Shining?"

"Right, I need to go offsite for that meeting. I'll be back after lunch."

He walked out of his top floor office and headed toward the courtyard. The day was sunny, with a teasing warm breeze. Summer would be here soon.

Syd met him by the fountain.

"GroupLeader! How goes the work?"

"Meetings, reports, and more meetings," Jon lamented.

"And this surprises you?"

Jon shook his head and said, "Not really. How is the prison refit going?

Syd snapped his fingers. "On track, on time. The Caverns, Underground Luxury Apartment Living', is a hit. All the units we've refitted so far have been sold. I've got people working three shifts to get the rest ready, and I've got merchants lining up for space in the Atrium commercial area."

"We've got conference centers, restaurants, art galleries, shops, auditoriums, and plenty of space to expand."

"For some reason, the apartments are really popular with the artist and musician crowd."

"But not for people who don't like tons of rock over their heads," said Jon.

"Meh. I couldn't live down there all the time, but to each his own. We do emphasize in the sales pitch about the geologic stability of the rock strata."

Jon grinned. "I bet. What about the Labyrinth and its occupants." Jon asked.

Syd cleared his throat. "Well, we captured most of the rebels down there, including this 'King' person. Most of the people we caught had outstanding criminal warrants against them, so we moved them to Imperium prisons. The others were included in the relocation/restitution project."

"You know, Jon, I was thinking that with all that open space, the Labyrinth would be ideal for an underground park. We've already got a tramway that connects the apartment complex to the geothermal station. It would be fairly cheap to landscape the area, and it could be used by both the residents and the geothermal station staff."

Jon said, "You really have a talent for urban planning."

Syd shrugged and said, "I just like my job. By the way, how is the geothermal project going?"

"I just met with Eva. She and her team have been invaluable."

"Nice looking lady, huh?" Syd grinned.

"You knew that she had, um, been restored?" said Jon.

"You need to pay more attention to your reports, GroupLeader." Syd teased.

"Yeah, you try keeping up with all that paperwork." Jon snorted.

Syd looked at him. "So, do you regret taking the job?"

Jon sighed. "No, of course not — I'm just still adjusting. Preparing for an economy where limitless energy is freely available is not as easy as it sounds."

Syd held up his hands. "Hey, I didn't say I wanted your job. Got any time off coming?"

Jon rubbed his face, "I've been so busy, I haven't given it much thought."

Syd said, "Let's get together later and knock around some ideas. Over dinner?"

Jon said, "Sounds like a plan. Listen, I've got to get back. Talk to you later."

As he returned to his office, Eema said, "GroupLeader, there's a man waiting to see you about a job. Do you know a Mr. Deemus?"